M000079465

The

Yellow Wallpaper

And Other Stories
The Complete Gothic Collection

By

Charlotte Perkins Gilman

Edited by Aric Cushing

This compilation is dedicated to Charlotte Perkins Gilman~ a woman with more than one voice.

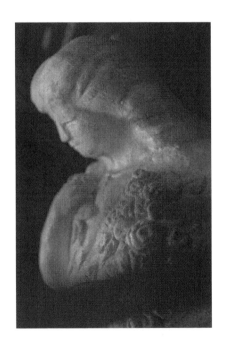

*Special thanks to Logan Thomas
for his extreme dedication
in helping to retrieve the otherwise lost
stories contained in this volume.*

The Yellow Wallpaper and Other Stories:
The Complete Gothic Collection

An Ascent Releasing Ent. Book
Published by Ascent Releasing Ent.
Copyright 2011 by Aric Cushing
All Rights Reserved
First Edition: November 2011

LIBRARY OF CONGRESS CATALOGING DATA
Cushing, Aric.
The Yellow Wallpaper and Other Stories:
The Complete Gothic Collection
ISBN-13: 978-0615568393
ISBN-10: 0615568394

The Yellow Wallpaper and Other Gothic Stories:
The Complete Gothic Collection / Aric Cushing /
Charlotte Perkins Gilman / All rights for contents belong
To Ascent Releasing Entertainment

Includes bibliographic references and index

Table of Contents

Is 'The Yellow Wallpaper' a Gothic Story?
By Aric Cushing

'*The Yellow Wallpaper*', and its well documented back story, has been galvanized by a movement—the women's movement. Even the history of its publication—Charlotte, after a severe bout of depression, went to see a Dr. Weir S. Mitchel, who then prescribed a 'rest cure' for her as prescription, exemplified (and still does) the prevalent social climate of patriarchal exclusion. The story encompasses numerous social elements, including feminism, but also possesses gothic horror elements as well, as noted by Gilman herself. The 'delicate' woman (or woman as 'invalid'), woman as possession, and the marginalizing of the narrator's opinions of her condition, obviously pre-conceptualizes Simone de Beauvoir's radical (at the time, and perhaps even today) novel, '*The Second Sex*', published in 1954. However, contrary to feminist interpretations, these themes are equally relevant as the gothic elements which also dominate the story. Gilman's first person narrative is woman as 'the Other' (de Beauvoir), and that for a woman to actually be 'free' from male specifications, madness is the only solution, whether outward or inward. Gilman's deliberate inclusion of the 'madness' theme, as well as the tonality of the story, no doubt contributed to her reformist ideas at the time. But, they also contributed to the gothic elements as well. By exploring the sociological perspective of a famous gothic novel (like *Dracula*), Gilman's true intent of the story can be explored. The story is both a criticism on the position of women in society, and, by Gilman's own admission, a gothic/horror story as well. By purposely weaving both societal comment with genre, Gilman succeeded in creating one of the greatest female-specific gothic stories of all time.

Before Gilman began publishing her Utopian work, her notable social reform stories, or her famous 'Women in Economics', her message of female independence was first conveyed in prose, the short story format, and essays. In regards to her fiction, at least in the late nineteenth century, Charlotte attempted to mix both fashion and faction. The few stories that she did write in the 'gothic' mode were a brief attempt to mix mood and mystery with the themes of female marginalization. Unsuited to her true purpose—the position of women in society and how to change it—Gilman quickly abandoned her gothic fiction for more direct social criticism. Her speeches, writings, stories, and tours were met with applause and disdain. Her then radical views regarding women's rights, freedoms, child rearing, and immigration, branded her as a radical, as well as rendered her indigent for many periods in her life. "You should consider more what the editors want," Theodore Dreiser told her (Gilman, pg. 304). Yes, the people wanted fiction. No, they did not want it mired in didacticism. Though Gilman turned away from the gothic/horror/ghost story as a means of storytelling, she nonetheless left readers with a variety of stories that served both feminists *and* genre enthusiasts.

Charlotte Perkins Gilman, born in 1860 to Frederick Beecher Perkins and Mary Fitch Westcott, wrote hundreds of poems, essays and short stories. Her career began with the publication of 'Similar Cases' (1890), which was published the same year she wrote 'The Yellow Wallpaper'. Though initially rejected, 'The Yellow Wallpaper' story was later published in the January edition of the New England Magazine in 1892. And though Gilman struggled her entire life for social reform, as evidenced by her notable works, *Herland*, and *With Her in Ourland*, (as well as her reknowned publication of *Women in Economics*), her most famous story still remains, undoubtedly, 'The Yellow Wallpaper'. To label Charlotte Perkins Gilman as a 'nationalist', which she was, or a 'socialist', which she wanted to be, or a feminist—the word as a political maneuvering had barely come into existence by this time, formulating around 1895—is not enough. She was a writer, and not just a reformist writer, but a writer of all types of fiction. And if 'The Yellow Wallpaper' had absolutely nothing to do with the gothic mode, as so many feminists and socialists proclaim, then why liken its' rejection to that of Edgar Allan Poe? "The story was meant to be dreadful, and succeeded. I suppose he (the agent Gilman submitted the story to) would have sent back one of Poe's on the same ground." (Gilman, pg. 119).

In 'The Yellow Wallpaper', the main character moves with her husband-doctor to a 'hereditary estate', labels the place as 'haunted', and takes the 'nursery at the top of the house' for a bedroom. There she encounters the 'hideous' yellow wallpaper which lulls her into doom and tricks her into freedom: a nursery that serves both as a surreal jail and an *Alice in Wonderland* escape. She is an invalid. A minor who must be looked after. She sees women 'creeping' behind the wallpaper—soon she is creeping. Creeping into a position of resignation. Not resignation to androcentric domination, but 'creeping' resignation to her inevitable freedom-based transformation. By the end of the story, the main character has transcended and physically mutated (her husband faints upon seeing her), into a raw, stripped (like the wallpaper), corset-free primeval woman. She cannot move the bed, so she gnaws on the bedpost. Afterwards, she strips the wallpaper. As the faces in the wallpaper pattern 'shriek with derision', one can imagine her standing in the suffocating nineteenth century room, clothes wet with perspiration, fingers bloody from work, eyes wild underneath a tangle of displaced hair. This image of a coffined, sealed-up woman, like the bloodied Lady Madeleineis in 'The Fall of the House of Usher', is an arresting gothic image — woman as demoniac earth-mother. It is Gilman's use of this image, at once so violent and shocking, that transcends the story far beyond the feminist perspective.

As in most of the gothic genre, the surroundings which trap the main character, also trap the main characters' soul. Charlotte Perkins Gilman used this symbology to link social alienation with the horrific. The main character of 'The Yellow Wallpaper', like Dracula (from Bram Stoker's novel, published in 1897) is destroyed by patriarchal determinism. They are sealed by their own history. The castle in which Dracula lives reflects the past, the nursery in 'The Yellow Wallpaper', a dead future. In Stoker's novel, Dracula does not want to see himself reflected. The image is too terrible. Conveniently, Stoker's story doesn't allow for the possibility, and Dracula's reflection is void. In 'The Yellow Wallpaper', the main character sees a woman behind the paper, and sometimes many women, but the shapes are vague and ghostly. They have no definition. Woman-kind and vampire-kind are only shadows, relegated to the same landscapes, and destroyed or dominated because of their nature.

Despite the wide variety of themes surrounding gothic literature, Gilman's use of woman as monster, which served well in double meaning for her reformist theories, dominates her gothic stories. In Edgar Allan Poe's 'The Fall of the House of Usher', woman as monster is used, as Charlotte Perkins Gilman's uses the theme, as symbol. In 'Usher', Lady Madeleineis is consigned immediately as wife and possession. In Gilman's 'The Rocking Chair', the story centers around the competition for consignment of a woman, and, like in 'Usher', the inevitable downfall of the men who are the source of this objectification.

Two friends enter a boarding establishment upon seeing a mysterious girl in a window, and 'the glory of her sunlit hair'. Upon staying in the dreary, strange house, both male friends attempt to court and attain an apparition—a ghost-woman whom, despite their efforts, constantly evades them in both speech and presence. The idea that she cannot be possessed does not cross their minds. Woman is to be conquered and *attained*, whether human or ghost. In Gilman's 'The Great Wistaria', this theme is continued. Not because the young girl in the beginning of the story is being pursued, but because she is already possessed by her father. By using the woman-as-monster theme, Gilman simul-taneously commented on how she felt herself to be viewed (by society), but also how she felt women viewed themselves. In most of Gilman's gothic stories, the fate of woman is deigned by their position in society. Only in 'The Yellow Wallpaper' is the reader allowed to identify with the heroine, live inside her mind, and experience the conflict as it unravels.

The publication of 'The Yellow Wallpaper' was a period in Gilman's life when she felt her social statements could be communicated quite effectively through the short story format. As Gilman's life progressed, so did her methods of conveyance. She shifted away from the narrative story and into a more commentative means of writing (along with lecturing and touring). In her autobiography, and after the publication of 'The Home', she wrote, ". . . during those four years, I had written The Home, which is the most heretical—and amusing—of anything I've done." (Gilman, pgs. 286-287). Unlike Charlotte's ex-husband, Walter Stetson, whose diaries were steeped in depression and guilt, Gilman's sense of humor was still in tact. While women were writing novels like 'The Perfect Woman' (Melendy, M.D., P.H.D.), and proclaiming "A high forehead is always to be admired, but if we don't possess it, then let us learn to so dress the head as to make what we have show to advantage" (Melendy, pg. 229) or statements like "Matrimony will indeed make a woman of her" (Melendy, pg. 43), Charlotte Perkins Gilman was revolutionizing the short story, the essay, the poem, and public speaking. Because her body of work is not specifically gothic, her position as an author in this genre should not be discarded. She did write stories with haunting and ghostly subtexts, but she also wrote with the specific intention of advancing the position of woman-kind in society. No other female gothic writer has accomplished this, even with the publication of larger bodies of work.

In 'The Yellow Wallpaper', the female narrator is *part* of the mystery, rooted in the ancient, and dominated because of it. What makes 'The Yellow Wallpaper' unique as a story is the rare example of both gothic *and* autobiographical perspective. In 'Frankenstein', Mary Wollstonecraft (also the writer of *The Vindication of the Rights of Woman*) wrote in the first person, but from the male point of view. Even the novelist Anne Rice, (though she drew from her own life to create *Interview with the Vampire* — Anne Rice's daughter died, which she reflected in the novel's character of Claudia) also predominantly writes from the male point of view. Perhaps to be taken seriously, or even considered, a woman must literally and figuratively *become* a man. Without this transformation, marginalization is imminent. Queen Elizabeth was no fool. Instead--in a time of Victorian manners and androcentric determinism--Charlotte Perkins Gilman lectured, wrote, and rebelled against the pervading position of her sex. Obviously, the greatest gothic literature is entrenched in social commentary, as evidenced by *Dracula* and *Frankenstein*. But, it is Gilman's exact use of this method, from a female point of view, as well as having an autobiographical slant and a dominating theme of 'woman as monster', that places Charlotte Perkins Gilman's *'The Yellow Wallpaper'* in the most unique category of all. A gothic story from the female point of view, without compromise.

She had the bravery to do it. And it worked.

The
Yellow Wallpaper

It is very seldom that mere ordinary people like John and myself secure ancestral halls for the summer.

A colonial mansion, a hereditary estate, I would say a haunted house, and reach the height of romantic felicity — but that would be asking too much of fate!

Still I will proudly declare that there is something queer about it.

Else, why should it be let so cheaply? And why have stood so long untenanted?

John laughs at me, of course, but one expects that in marriage.

John is practical in the extreme. He has no patience with faith, an intense horror of superstition, and he scoffs openly at any talk of things not to be felt and seen and put down in figures.

John is a physician, and PERHAPS — (I would not say it to a living soul, of course, but this is dead paper and a great relief to my mind) — PERHAPS that is one reason I do not get well faster.

You see he does not believe I am sick!

And what can one do?

If a physician of high standing, and one's own husband, assures friends and relatives that there is really nothing the matter with one but temporary nervous depression — a slight hysterical tendency — what is one to do?

My brother is also a physician, and also of high standing, and he says the same thing.

So I take phosphates or phosphites — whichever it is, and tonics, and journeys, and air, and exercise, and am absolutely forbidden to "work" until I am well again.

Personally, I disagree with their ideas.

Personally, I believe that congenial work, with excitement and change, would do me good.

But what is one to do?

I did write for a while in spite of them; but it DOES exhaust me a good deal — having to be so sly about it, or else meet with heavy opposition.

I sometimes fancy that my condition if I had less opposition and more society and stimulus — but John says the very worst thing I can do is to think about my condition, and I confess it always makes me feel bad.

So I will let it alone and talk about the house.

The most beautiful place! It is quite alone, standing well back from the road, quite three miles from the village. It makes me think of English places that you read about, for there are hedges and walls and gates that lock, and lots of separate little houses for the gardeners and people.

There is a DELICIOUS garden! I never saw such a garden—large and shady, full of box-bordered paths, and lined with long grape-covered arbors with seats under them.

There were greenhouses, too, but they are all broken now.

There was some legal trouble, I believe, something about the heirs and coheirs; anyhow, the place has been empty for years.

That spoils my ghostliness, I am afraid, but I don't care—there is something strange about the house—I can feel it.

I even said so to John one moonlight evening, but he said what I felt was a DRAUGHT, and shut the window.

I get unreasonably angry with John sometimes. I'm sure I never used to be so sensitive. I think it is due to this nervous condition.

But John says if I feel so, I shall neglect proper self-control; so I take pains to control myself—before him, at least, and that makes me very tired.

I don't like our room a bit. I wanted one downstairs that opened on the piazza and had roses all over the window, and such pretty old-fashioned chintz hangings! but John would not hear of it.

~

He said there was only one window and not room for two beds, and no near room for him if he took another.

He is very careful and loving, and hardly lets me stir without special direction.

I have a schedule prescription for each hour in the day; he takes all care from me, and so I feel basely ungrateful not to value it more.

He said we came here solely on my account, that I was to have perfect rest and all the air I could get. "Your exercise depends on your strength, my dear," said he, "and your food somewhat on your appetite; but air you can absorb all the time." So we took the nursery at the top of the house.

It is a big, airy room, the whole floor nearly, with windows that look all ways, and air and sunshine galore. It was nursery first and then playroom and gymnasium, I should judge; for the windows are barred for little children, and there are rings and things in the walls.

The paint and paper look as if a boys' school had used it. It is stripped off—the paper—in great patches all around the head of my bed, about as far as I can reach, and in a great place on the other side of the room low down. I never saw a worse paper in my life.

One of those sprawling flamboyant patterns committing every artistic sin.

It is dull enough to confuse the eye in following, pronounced enough to constantly irritate and provoke study, and when you follow the lame uncertain curves for a little distance they suddenly commit suicide—plunge off at outrageous angles, destroy themselves in unheard of contradictions.

The color is repellent, almost revolting; a smouldering unclean yellow, strangely faded by the slow-turning sunlight.

It is a dull yet lurid orange in some places, a sickly sulphur tint in others.

No wonder the children hated it! I should hate it myself if I had to live in this room long.

There comes John, and I must put this away,—he hates to have me write a word.

We have been here two weeks, and I haven't felt like writing before, since that first day.

~

I am sitting by the window now, up in this atrocious nursery, and there is nothing to hinder my writing as much as I please, save lack of strength.

John is away all day, and even some nights when his cases are serious.

I am glad my case is not serious!

But these nervous troubles are dreadfully depressing.

John does not know how much I really suffer. He knows there is no REASON to suffer, and that satisfies him.

Of course it is only nervousness. It does weigh on me so not to do my duty in any way!

I meant to be such a help to John, such a real rest and comfort, and here I am a comparative burden already!

Nobody would believe what an effort it is to do what little I am able, — to dress and entertain, and other things.

It is fortunate Mary is so good with the baby. Such a dear baby!

And yet I CANNOT be with him, it makes me so

nervous.

I suppose John never was nervous in his life. He laughs at me so about this wall-paper!

At first he meant to repaper the room, but afterwards he said that I was letting it get the better of me, and that nothing was worse for a nervous patient than to give way to such fancies.

He said that after the wall-paper was changed it would be the heavy bedstead, and then the barred windows, and then that gate at the head of the stairs, and so on.

"You know the place is doing you good," he said, "and really, dear, I don't care to renovate the house just for a three months' rental."

"Then do let us go downstairs," I said, "there are such pretty rooms there."

Then he took me in his arms and called me a blessed little goose, and said he would go down to the cellar, if I wished, and have it whitewashed into the bargain.

But he is right enough about the beds and windows and things.

It is an airy and comfortable room as any one need wish, and of course, I would not be so silly as to make him uncomfortable just for a whim.

I'm really getting quite fond of the big room, all but that horrid paper.

Out of one window I can see the garden, those mysterious deepshaded arbors, the riotous old-fashioned flowers, and bushes and gnarly trees.

Out of another I get a lovely view of the bay and a little private wharf belonging to the estate. There is a beautiful shaded lane that runs down there from the house. I always fancy I see people walking in these numerous paths and arbors, but John has cautioned me not to give way to fancy in the least. He says that with my imaginative power and habit of story-making, a nervous weakness like mine is sure to lead to all manner of excited fancies, and that I ought to use my will and good sense to check the tendency. So I try.

I think sometimes that if I were only well enough to write a little it would relieve the press of ideas and rest me.

But I find I get pretty tired when I try.

It is so discouraging not to have any advice and companionship about my work. When I get really well, John says we will ask Cousin Henry and Julia down for a long visit; but he says he would as soon put fireworks in my pillow-case as to let me have those stimulating people about now.

I wish I could get well faster.

But I must not think about that. This paper looks to me as if it KNEW what a vicious influence it had!

There is a recurrent spot where the pattern lolls like a broken neck and two bulbous eyes stare at you upside down.

I get positively angry with the impertinence of it and the everlastingness. Up and down and sideways they crawl, and those absurd, unblinking eyes are everywhere. There is one place where two breadths didn't match, and the eyes go all up and down the line, one a little higher than the other.

I never saw so much expression in an inanimate thing before, and we all know how much expression they have! I used to lie awake as a child and get more entertainment and terror out of blank walls and plain furniture than most children could find in a toy store.

I remember what a kindly wink the knobs of our big, old bureau used to have, and there was one chair that always seemed like a strong friend.

I used to feel that if any of the other things looked too fierce I could always hop into that chair and be safe.

The furniture in this room is no worse than inharmonious, however, for we had to bring it all from downstairs. I suppose when this was used as a playroom they had to take the nursery things out, and no wonder! I never saw such ravages as the children have made here.

The wall-paper, as I said before, is torn off in spots, and it sticketh closer than a brother—they must have had perseverance as well as hatred.

Then the floor is scratched and gouged and splintered, the plaster itself is dug out here and there, and this great heavy bed which is all we found in the room, looks as if it had been through the wars.

But I don't mind it a bit—only the paper.

There comes John's sister. Such a dear girl as she is, and so careful of me! I must not let her find me writing.

She is a perfect and enthusiastic housekeeper, and hopes for no better profession. I verily believe she thinks it is the writing which made me sick!

But I can write when she is out, and see her a long way off from these windows. There is one that commands the road, a lovely shaded winding road, and one that just looks off over the country. A lovely country, too, full of great elms and velvet meadows.

This wall-paper has a kind of sub-pattern in a different shade, a particularly irritating one, for you can only see it in certain lights, and not clearly then.

But in the places where it isn't faded and where the sun is just so—I can see a strange, provoking, formless sort of figure, that seems to skulk about behind that silly and conspicuous front design.

There's sister on the stairs!

~

Well, the Fourth of July is over! The people are gone and I am tired out. John thought it might do me good to see a little company, so we just had mother and Nellie and the children down for a week.

Of course I didn't do a thing. Jennie sees to everything now.

But it tired me all the same.

John says if I don't pick up faster he shall send me to Weir Mitchell in the fall.

But I don't want to go there at all. I had a friend who was in his hands once, and she says he is just like John and my brother, only more so!

Besides, it is such an undertaking to go so far.

I don't feel as if it was worth while to turn my hand over for anything, and I'm getting dreadfully fretful and querulous.

I cry at nothing, and cry most of the time.

Of course I don't when John is here, or anybody else, but when I am alone.

And I am alone a good deal just now. John is kept in town very often by serious cases, and Jennie is good and lets me alone when I want her to.

So I walk a little in the garden or down that lovely lane, sit on the porch under the roses, and lie down up here a good deal.

I'm getting really fond of the room in spite of the wall-paper.

Perhaps BECAUSE of the wall-paper.

It dwells in my mind so!

I lie here on this great immovable bed—it is nailed down, I believe—and follow that pattern about by the hour. It is as good as gymnastics, I assure you. I start, we'll say, at the bottom, down in the corner over there where it has not been touched, and I determine for the thousandth time that I WILL follow that pointless pattern to some sort of a conclusion.

I know a little of the principle of design, and I know this thing was not arranged on any laws of radiation, or alternation, or repetition, or symmetry, or anything else that I ever heard of.

It is repeated, of course, by the breadths, but not otherwise.

Looked at in one way each breadth stands alone, the bloated curves and flourishes—a kind of "debased Romanesque" with delirium tremens—go waddling up and down in isolated columns of fatuity.

But, on the other hand, they connect diagonally, and the sprawling outlines run off in great slanting waves of optic horror, like a lot of wallowing seaweeds in full chase.

The whole thing goes horizontally, too, at least it seems so, and I exhaust myself in trying to distinguish the order of its going in that direction.

They have used a horizontal breadth for a frieze, and that adds wonderfully to the confusion.

There is one end of the room where it is almost intact, and there, when the crosslights fade and the low sun shines directly upon it, I can almost fancy radiation after all, — the interminable grotesques seem to form around a common centre and rush off in headlong plunges of equal distraction.

It makes me tired to follow it. I will take a nap I guess.

~

I don't know why I should write this.

I don't want to.

I don't feel able.

And I know John would think it absurd. But I MUST say what I feel and think in some way — it is such a relief!

But the effort is getting to be greater than the relief.

Half the time now I am awfully lazy, and lie down ever so much.

John says I musn't lose my strength, and has me take cod liver oil and lots of tonics and things, to say nothing of ale and wine and rare meat.

Dear John! He loves me very dearly, and hates to have me sick. I tried to have a real earnest reasonable talk with him the other day, and tell him how I wish he would let me go and make a visit to Cousin Henry and Julia.

But he said I wasn't able to go, nor able to stand it after I got there; and I did not make out a very good case for myself, for I was crying before I had finished.

It is getting to be a great effort for me to think straight. Just this nervous weakness I suppose.

And dear John gathered me up in his arms, and just carried me upstairs and laid me on the bed, and sat by me and read to me till it tired my head.

He said I was his darling and his comfort and all he had, and that I must take care of myself for his sake, and keep well.

He says no one but myself can help me out of it, that I must use my will and self-control and not let any silly fancies run away with me.

There's one comfort, the baby is well and happy, and does not have to occupy this nursery with the horrid wall-paper.

If we had not used it, that blessed child would have! What a fortunate escape! Why, I wouldn't have a child of mine, an impressionable little thing, live in such a room for worlds.

I never thought of it before, but it is lucky that John kept me here after all, I can stand it so much easier than a baby, you see.

Of course I never mention it to them any more—I am too wise,—but I keep watch of it all the same.

There are things in that paper that nobody knows but me, or ever will.

Behind that outside pattern the dim shapes get clearer every day.

It is always the same shape, only very numerous.

And it is like a woman stooping down and creeping about behind that pattern. I don't like it a bit. I wonder—I begin to think—I wish John would take me away from here!

It is so hard to talk with John about my case, because he is so wise, and because he loves me so.

But I tried it last night.

It was moonlight. The moon shines in all around just as the sun does.

I hate to see it sometimes, it creeps so slowly, and always comes in by one window or another.

John was asleep and I hated to waken him, so I kept still and watched the moonlight on that undulating wall-paper till I felt creepy.

The faint figure behind seemed to shake the pattern, just as if she wanted to get out.

I got up softly and went to feel and see if the paper DID move, and when I came back John was awake.

"What is it, little girl?" he said. "Don't go walking about like that—you'll get cold."

I thought it was a good time to talk, so I told him that I really was not gaining here, and that I wished he would take me away.

"Why darling!" said he, "our lease will be up in three weeks, and I can't see how to leave before.

"The repairs are not done at home, and I cannot possibly leave town just now. Of course if you were in any danger, I could and would, but you really are better, dear, whether you can see it or not. I am a doctor, dear, and I know. You are gaining flesh and color, your appetite is better, I feel really much easier about you."

"I don't weigh a bit more," said I, "nor as much; and my appetite may be better in the evening when you are here, but it is worse in the morning when you are away!"

"Bless her little heart!" said he with a big hug, "she shall be as sick as she pleases! But now let's improve the shining hours by going to sleep, and talk about it in the morning!"

"And you won't go away?" I asked gloomily.

"Why, how can I, dear? It is only three weeks more and then we will take a nice little trip of a few days while Jennie is getting the house ready. Really dear you are better!"

"Better in body perhaps—" I began, and stopped short, for he sat up straight and looked at me with such a stern, reproachful look that I could not say another word.

"My darling," said he, "I beg of you, for my sake and for our child's sake, as well as for your own, that you will never for one instant let that idea enter your mind! There is nothing so dangerous, so fascinating, to a temperament like yours. It is a false and foolish fancy. Can you not trust me as a physician when I tell you so?"

So of course I said no more on that score, and we went to sleep before long. He thought I was asleep first, but I wasn't, and lay there for hours trying to decide whether that front pattern and the back pattern really did move together or separately.

~

On a pattern like this, by daylight, there is a lack of sequence, a defiance of law, that is a constant irritant to a normal mind.

The color is hideous enough, and unreliable enough, and infuriating enough, but the pattern is torturing.

You think you have mastered it, but just as you get well underway in following, it turns a back-somersault and there you are. It slaps you in the face, knocks you down, and tramples upon you. It is like a bad dream.

The outside pattern is a florid arabesque, reminding one of a fungus. If you can imagine a toadstool in joints, an interminable string of toadstools, budding and sprouting in endless convolutions — why, that is something like it.

That is, sometimes!

There is one marked peculiarity about this paper, a thing nobody seems to notice but myself, and that is that it changes as the light changes.

When the sun shoots in through the east window — I always watch for that first long, straight ray — it changes so quickly that I never can quite believe it.

That is why I watch it always.

By moonlight — the moon shines in all night when there is a moon — I wouldn't know it was the same paper.

At night in any kind of light, in twilight, candle light, lamplight, and worst of all by moonlight, it becomes bars! The outside pattern I mean, and the woman behind it is as plain as can be. I didn't realize for a long time what the thing was that showed behind, that dim sub-pattern, but now I am quite sure it is a woman.

By daylight she is subdued, quiet. I fancy it is the pattern that keeps her so still. It is so puzzling. It keeps me quiet by the hour.

I lie down ever so much now. John says it is good for me, and to sleep all I can.

Indeed he started the habit by making me lie down for an hour after each meal.

It is a very bad habit I am convinced, for you see I don't sleep.

And that cultivates deceit, for I don't tell them I'm awake — O no!

The fact is I am getting a little afraid of John.

He seems very queer sometimes, and even Jennie has an inexplicable look.

It strikes me occasionally, just as a scientific hypothesis, — that perhaps it is the paper!

I have watched John when he did not know I was looking, and come into the room suddenly on the most innocent excuses, and I've caught him several times LOOKING AT THE PAPER! And Jennie too. I caught Jennie with her hand on it once.

She didn't know I was in the room, and when I asked her in a quiet, a very quiet voice, with the most restrained manner possible, what she was doing with the paper — she turned around as if she had been caught stealing, and looked quite angry — asked me why I should frighten her so!

Then she said that the paper stained everything it touched, that she had found yellow smooches on all my clothes and John's, and she wished we would be more careful!

Did not that sound innocent? But I know she was studying that pattern, and I am determined that nobody shall find it out but myself!

Life is very much more exciting now than it used to be. You see I have something more to expect, to look forward to, to watch. I really do eat better, and am more quiet than I was.

John is so pleased to see me improve! He laughed a little the other day, and said I seemed to be flourishing in spite of my wall-paper.

I turned it off with a laugh. I had no intention of telling him it was BECAUSE of the wall-paper—he would make fun of me. He might even want to take me away.

I don't want to leave now until I have found it out. There is a week more, and I think that will be enough.

~

I'm feeling ever so much better! I don't sleep much at night, for it is so interesting to watch developments; but I sleep a good deal in the daytime.

In the daytime it is tiresome and perplexing.

There are always new shoots on the fungus, and new shades of yellow all over it. I cannot keep count of them, though I have tried conscientiously.

It is the strangest yellow, that wall-paper! It makes me think of all the yellow things I ever saw—not beautiful ones like buttercups, but old foul, bad yellow things.

But there is something else about that paper—the smell! I noticed it the moment we came into the room, but with so much air and sun it was not bad. Now we have had a week of fog and rain, and whether the windows are open or not, the smell is here.

It creeps all over the house.

I find it hovering in the dining-room, skulking in the parlor, hiding in the hall, lying in wait for me on the stairs.

It gets into my hair.

Even when I go to ride, if I turn my head suddenly and surprise it—there is that smell!

Such a peculiar odor, too! I have spent hours in trying to analyze it, to find what it smelled like.

It is not bad—at first, and very gentle, but quite the subtlest, most enduring odor I ever met.

In this damp weather it is awful, I wake up in the night and find it hanging over me.

It used to disturb me at first. I thought seriously of burning the house—to reach the smell.

But now I am used to it. The only thing I can think of that it is like is the COLOR of the paper! A yellow smell.

There is a very funny mark on this wall, low down, near the mopboard.

A streak that runs round the room. It goes behind every piece of furniture, except the bed, a long, straight, even SMOOCH, as if it had been rubbed over and over.

I wonder how it was done and who did it, and what they did it for. Round and round and round—round and round and round—it makes me dizzy!

I really have discovered something at last.

Through watching so much at night, when it changes so, I have finally found out.

The front pattern DOES move—and no wonder! The woman behind shakes it!

Sometimes I think there a great many women behind, and sometimes only one, and she crawls around fast, and her crawling shakes it all over.

Then in the very bright spots she keeps still, and in the

very shady spots she just takes hold of the bars and shakes them hard.

And she is all the time trying to climb through. But nobody could climb through that pattern—it strangles so; I think that is why it has so many heads.

They get through, and then the pattern strangles them off and turns them upside down, and makes their eyes white!

If those heads were covered or taken off it would not be half so bad.

~

I think that woman gets out in the daytime!

And I'll tell you why—privately—I've seen her!

I can see her out of every one of my windows!

It is the same woman, I know, for she is always creeping, and most women do not creep by daylight.

I see her on that long road under the trees, creeping along, and when a carriage comes she hides under the blackberry vines.

I don't blame her a bit. It must be very humiliating to be caught creeping by daylight!

I always lock the door when I creep by daylight. I can't do it at night, for I know John would suspect something at once.

And John is so queer now, that I don't want to irritate him. I wish he would take another room! Besides, I don't want anybody to get that woman out at night but myself.

I often wonder if I could see her out of all the windows at once.

But, turn as fast as I can, I can only see out of one at a time.

And though I always see her, she MAY be able to creep faster than I can turn!

I have watched her sometimes away off in the open country, creeping as fast as a cloud shadow in a high wind.

~

If only that top pattern could be gotten off from the under one! I mean to try it, little by little.

I have found out another funny thing, but I shan't tell it this time! It does not do to trust people too much.

There are only two more days to get this paper off, and I believe John is beginning to notice. I don't like the look in his eyes.

And I heard him ask Jennie a lot of professional questions about me. She had a very good report to give.

She said I slept a good deal in the daytime.

John knows I don't sleep very well at night, for all I'm so quiet!

He asked me all sorts of questions, too, and pretended to be very loving and kind.

As if I couldn't see through him!

Still, I don't wonder he acts so, sleeping under this paper for three months.

It only interests me, but I feel sure John and Jennie are secretly affected by it.

~

Hurrah! This is the last day, but it is enough. John is to stay in town over night, and won't be out until this evening.

Jennie wanted to sleep with me—the sly thing! But I told her I should undoubtedly rest better for a night all alone.

That was clever, for really I wasn't alone a bit! As soon as it was moonlight and that poor thing began to crawl and shake the pattern, I got up and ran to help her.

I pulled and she shook, I shook and she pulled, and before morning we had peeled off yards of that paper.

A strip about as high as my head and half around the room.

And then when the sun came and that awful pattern began to laugh at me, I declared I would finish it to-day!

We go away to-morrow, and they are moving all my furniture down again to leave things as they were before.

Jennie looked at the wall in amazement, but I told her merrily that I did it out of pure spite at the vicious thing.

She laughed and said she wouldn't mind doing it herself, but I must not get tired.

How she betrayed herself that time!

But I am here, and no person touches this paper but me—not ALIVE!

She tried to get me out of the room—it was too patent! But I said it was so quiet and empty and clean now that I believed I would lie down again and sleep all I could; and not to wake me even for dinner—I would call when I woke.

So now she is gone, and the servants are gone, and the things are gone, and there is nothing left but that great bedstead nailed down, with the canvas mattress we found on it.

We shall sleep downstairs to-night, and take the boat home tomorrow.

I quite enjoy the room, now it is bare again.

How those children did tear about here!

This bedstead is fairly gnawed!

But I must get to work.

I have locked the door and thrown the key down into the front path.

I don't want to go out, and I don't want to have anybody come in, till John comes.

I want to astonish him.

I've got a rope up here that even Jennie did not find. If that woman does get out, and tries to get away, I can tie her!

But I forgot I could not reach far without anything to stand on!

This bed will NOT move!

I tried to lift and push it until I was lame, and then I got so angry I bit off a little piece at one corner—but it hurt my teeth.

Then I peeled off all the paper I could reach standing on the floor. It sticks horribly and the pattern just enjoys it! All those strangled heads and bulbous eyes and waddling fungus growths just shriek with derision!

I am getting angry enough to do something desperate. To jump out of the window would be admirable exercise, but the bars are too strong even to try.

Besides I wouldn't do it. Of course not. I know well enough that a step like that is improper and might be misconstrued.

I don't like to LOOK out of the windows even—there are so many of those creeping women, and they creep so fast.

I wonder if they all come out of that wall-paper as I did?

But I am securely fastened now by my well-hidden rope—you don't get ME out in the road there!

I suppose I shall have to get back behind the pattern when it comes night, and that is hard!

It is so pleasant to be out in this great room and creep around as I please!

I don't want to go outside. I won't, even if Jennie asks me to.

For outside you have to creep on the ground, and everything is green instead of yellow.

But here I can creep smoothly on the floor, and my shoulder just fits in that long smooch around the wall, so I cannot lose my way.

Why there's John at the door!

It is no use, young man, you can't open it!

How he does call and pound!

Now he's crying for an axe.

It would be a shame to break down that beautiful door!

"John dear!" said I in the gentlest voice, "the key is down by the front steps, under a plantain leaf!"

That silenced him for a few moments.

Then he said—very quietly indeed, "Open the door, my darling!"

"I can't," said I. "The key is down by the front door

under a plantain leaf!"

And then I said it again, several times, very gently and slowly, and said it so often that he had to go and see, and he got it of course, and came in. He stopped short by the door.

"What is the matter?" he cried. "For God's sake, what are you doing!"

I kept on creeping just the same, but I looked at him over my shoulder.

"I've got out at last," said I, "in spite of you and Jane. And I've pulled off most of the paper, so you can't put me back!"

Now why should that man have fainted? But he did, and right across my path by the wall, so that I had to creep over him every time!

The

Unwatched Door

I sat calmly in my marble house and none knew what was under it or who had put it there. The house was very beautiful, I knew that. I had engaged the best of architects and builders, the materials were of spotless purity, and every block cost a great sum. Around it the flowers grew, rich, brilliant flowers, in eddying sweeps of color that pulsed and flowed up to the white walls, over the wide steps, and out into the vivid velvet of the lawn. Flowers I would have, and not only those in the rich beds — the soil was very fertile where I built my house — but in exuberant vines which grew up against both wall and window and overhung the gleaming porch with their dripping crimson bells and buds.

The trees were not very tall yet, not tall enough to give the place the air I wanted, and some which I had eagerly transplanted died after a little while and stood withered and stiff among the flowers. But even those the vines soon covered, riotous climbing things that shot out creeping fingers of pale delicate green, which turned to clutching hands, and then to embracing arms that only death would loosen.

My house was full of beautiful and curious things; memorials of past ages and other lands, and specimens or strange unusual growths and freaks — a wonderful collection. But the strangest thing of all, and one I could not myself account for, was a singular low sound I heard sometimes among my curiosities. A low, faint, irregular, throbbing sound.

I lived there in a free and noble manner, well served and respected, but I had few friends to dwell in the house and love it. It almost seemed to me sometimes as if they knew what was under the house and who had put it there.

The Prince of that country came riding by one day and found me tending my flowers with passionate devotion. I watched over them as a mother watches her children; and when all the air was golden and crimson and purple and scarlet with their uncounted blossoms I was satisfied. My home looked joyous then.

The Prince was interested in my flowers. He used to dismount and stand there on the porch, leaning against a pillar of red porphyry, watching my white fingers disentangle the clinging tendrills and lead them to a higher, firmer hold on the rich carving. I wanted my house to be hidden flowers. Then he asked to see the inside of it and I led him in. He was welcome to go in as out and he liked, and, if he cared to know, I would explain to him all the curious things I kept there. I knew them all, just where they came from, what they were, and how they became mine, and solely mine. So I looked at him with cold eyes and told him all he asked about my household goods.

"It is a beautiful house," he said, "and over rich with flowers. But you—you seem sad."

Then I laughed, quietly, to show that I was not sad; for it was not indeed melancholy that affected me, as I lived in this fair house among the ruddy roses and thick, sweet lilies; only an interest in the place and a pride in it. For no one had so fair and firm and well built a house as I, nor one so buried in beauty.

But the Prince persisted that I was indeed unhappy. He missed something, he said, in all the beauty and lightness, and something in the tales I told him of my gathering these strange things. There were things there, he said, that seemed to call for another explanation than the one I had given—things that seemed to call for another ownership.

Then suddenly he held out his hands to me, with deep eyes searching mine.

"Show me your heart!" he said.

A faintness that was like pain ran through me at his words — it seemed as if the house shook under my feet, and in the demanding silence I caught that sound I could not myself account for, among the jars and cases around us both. But I held my head high and met his gaze as calmly as if he were but one of my strange idols; and I drew in deep breaths of sweetness from the drooping wreaths of jasmine that hung over the window close.

"I have none" said I.

He came close to me then with a look of doubt and terror, and laid his hand above my girdle, my straight silver girdle with the curious intricate clasp no one knew but myself. But he felt nothing, nothing, and I laughed softly at the anguish in his eyes.

Then he looked again at the cabinet next him and seemed to be counting over some of the things there. I sought to draw his attention away from them by my usual explanation, but he would not hear me. A wreath of withered roses in a dim corner of the case seemed to stimulate him anew, for he suddenly turned upon me again and demanded, "Where is your heart? What have you done with it?"

I trembled before him, for we were alone and the heavy, fragrant twilight was settling down. But his eyes burned steadily and he seized me by both wrists and bore me backward to the wall.

"What have you done with your heart?" said he.

Then a horrible pain ran through me in all the empty places, and I threw back my head and laughed long and loud, laughed madly, wildly.

Of what use was his fury and persistence? He could not have what he asked for, ever.

"If you must know," said I, "my heart is dead. Quite dead. It died many years ago."

"Are you sure it is dead?" said he with a deep, searching

tenderness that made me shiver. "Hearts have been known to lie long as dead; yet revive when One comes to touch them. Let me see your heart. Let me touch it."

I shook off his hand and smiled coldly, cruelly.

"My heart is really dead," I answered. "To make sure, I myself drove deeper every stroke that slew it. I sealed it in linen and folded it in lead. I laid it in a stone coffin, a monolith, bound with iron. I buried it under seven vaults and built this fair house over it; my fair, bright house where flowers grow so wild."

"Why did you build your house over the tomb?" he asked.

"That none might know there was a tomb," I answered coldly.

"Have you watched the door?" said he.

"Watched the door!" I cried, clutching at my cold breast, "watched the door of a tomb? Why should I? A tomb is not a prison!"

But even as I spoke a horrible thought seized me and I broke from him and ran leaping down the stairs that led below.

He followed me eagerly, his sword clanking on the wide, damp steps where no sound had fallen for so long.

I sought to bar the doors behind me, but he always caught my hand in time and passed through by my side.

At first I thought I caught again the low sound I knew above, but it had stopped wholly now, and as I turned to face him at the last door, my face white with terror, there was no breath of sound, no pulse of motion anywhere.

"Oh go away!" I moaned — go away utterly and let me look. You shall not see — you shall not touch — O my heart! My little heart that died so long ago! Go from me, you torture me — I tell you my heard is dead!"

But he never moved his steady eyes.

"Open the door," said he.

Then I opened the door. Dark—dark till our swinging lanterns struck faintly into the cold gloom. The great sarcophagus loomed dim and black in the middle. A scent of flowers years dead hung over it. But what was that—that little crouching thing that suddenly sprang up and ran upon us with unearthly eyes—on us—over us like an escaping beast, up the echoing stairs and out into the hot, sweet night with frantic leaps and wavering senseless cries. My heart was mad.

Clifford's Tower

There are few localities in New England where so much of the charm and color of old romance was given to the landscape by the work of man, as that which lay under the far reaching and dignified shadow of Clifford's Tower. The houses in the neighboring village were of no nobler character than those of any similar group of human habitations in all the country-side; neither were the lives of the citizens—if indeed we can designate with so large a title the humble dwellers in this hamlet—more dignified nor more ambitious than were those of their fellows. None the less was there a certain air of pride in the bearing of any resident when you asked him concerning the battlemented grandeur that stood so dark and tall against the evening sky. "That," you would have been told, with an unconscious arrogance in the tone of the speaker, "that is Clifford's Tower."

The Cliffords, it further appeared, were a great family in that place. They had been a great family when old Sir Mortimer Clifford received his grant of New World land from a king of whom the envious did say that he was glad to so cheaply ride himself of a too officious servant; and they were a great family now, still holding wide lands in the very heart of this fair and fertile region, and mighty industries which made them arbiters of fate to the greater part of the population.

True, some of the house of Clifford were not so great and powerful, not so prosperous and full of success, as were the main branch; yet every last bough and twig felt to the full the Clifford pride, and gloried daily in that standing record of past magnificence — Clifford's Tower. Of these poorer yet no humbler Cliffords, none were more pronounced in the characteristics of their race than Mistress Catharine Clifford and her fair daughter. Agnes Clifford knew by heart the story of her kinsman of old days-that young, proud, handsome Clifford who had traversed the four seas and levied tribute on all lands, to make fair and rich the great manor to which he was to bring home to his bride. He had planted those wide acres with every tree and shrub the climate would allow — strange vines and unknown bushes, flowers from across the world-and in the midst of them he reared the walls of this gray tower, meaning to have there a manor house which should rival in this new world the ancestral glory of his family in the old.

It was no fit match for a Clifford after all; this wild slip of a country lass he had chosen for a wife, a fair maiden enough, and virtuous, although her father was only a sea captain and her heart, the gossips said, was buried at sea with her first love. But Herndon Clifford loved fair Mabel Hurd all the better that she was cold and hard to win, and the more his family showed scorn of her whom he had chosen, the more he sought to exalt her by every high observance. She should have home such as no other lady in the land could claim, not even a Clifford; he would make for her a castle, not a house; and then as the day drew for the completion of the building and hid happiness, the sea gave up its dead — and there returned to her the lover she had mourned so long. Herdon Clifford stopped the work on the house and the work on the place at once; and all these the gray stone tower had looked down on the unfinished walls beside it and the tangled waste of strange dark foliage below — a ruin that had never been a home; whose master wandered in far lands, an exile till he died. The Clifford pride would never sell or let the grand demesne, a broken heart might be carried with unmoved countenance, a life might pass in sorrow, but the tower stood.

And when Agnes Clifford, fair pale Agnes whose short life was passed in the very shadow of the tower—for her mother had found shelter after a stormy youth under the roof of the never finished home beside it,-when Agnes first met a lover, it was in these long whispering avenues of strange trees, and in sheltered nooks where flowers bloomed rankly, large flowers of a sort unknown to the land about.

Urgent and warm was his wooing, and he begged her to leave these sickly shadows, this dark world of green and gray and come to the cheery light of his cottage on the hillside. "The sun shines there all day," he said to her, "and there are scarlet-flowered bean vines that drum merrily on the pane in the fresh sea winds. You know my sister already, and love her; she will be company for you while I am on the bay." For Robert Hurd was a fisherman as his father and grandfather had been before him, --and he prospered in a sturdy quiet way. His sister Elsie, a blithe and wholesome lass whose bright checks had the fresh color of sea pinks in them, kept house for him in the new cottage he had built; and to his cheery home he sought to lead the slender, drooping maiden, whose very life seemed colored by the darkness of the tangled trees about her, and the shadow of the tower.

"Come, Agnes" urged her lover. "You need more air, more light. The wind never stirs under these matted boughs-it only shakes the gathered fog down on the house and on you. The sun does not get in—see—look at the green moss on the side of every trunk—on the roof—here even by the doorsteps—and all down the tower—come! Bring your mother with you, we will cheer her in spite of herself. She cannot live long here."

"Agnes! Come here!" cried a weak, harsh voice from within. "Come here, and bring that man to me!"

Agnes obeyed, and her tall lover followed, his broad shoulders and ruddy cheeks bearing a sense of youth and strength into the shadowy room where age and illness lay.

Mistress Catharine Clifford lay back upon the pillows, as she had lain for long years past, her firm thin lips and clear eyes telling of an undiminished will which had once ruled many, but whose only instrument now was this one pale girl.

"Agnes!" said she "What is this? What is this young man to you?"

He spoke for her at once.

"Mistress Catharine Clifford," said he firmly, " I am come to ask your daughter's hand, and to offer her and you a home which will be more fit for human use than this. I love her well and can keep her, if not in grandeur, at least in loving comfort. You will not deny us your consent?"

The sick woman's eyes burned large and fierce as she listened, and she fixed them on him with scorn so deep that gentle Agnes was roused to immediate, quick rebellion.

"You shall not look at him so !" she cried. "He is a good man, mother and I love him!" Her mother turned her gaze on her daughter, with the same relentless scorn.

"You love him, do you? You love him? You, a Clifford, love this Hurd! And do know that he is but the grandson of that Mabel Hurd for whose false faith this great house stands today unbuilt! He says it is unfit for human use, this house which should have been the glory of the country had that girl been true! But a Clifford was well served for loving so beneath him; and you shall fare no better if you love this man. You, a Clifford, living here on your own land, to wed a fisherman and go to live in his cheap hut—and offer *me* a home! Thank God your mother lives and can defend you yet from the weakness of your heart! Thank God that in my very helplessness I hold you fast. You cannot leave me for a day—a night—and while I live, and while this tower shall stand, you shall not marry this man!"

A sudden darkness gathered while she spoke. In those green shades the dark came earlier always, but this fell thickly as though a curtain closed across the sky.

Not a leaf stirred; the insistent shrilling of insects filled the hot air with vibrant energy. Far off a heavy breath of sound and the soft sheeted flashes of heat lightning spoke of a gathering storm.

Robert Hurd stood pale and silent, then turned and strode away without a word. Agnes followed him to the door. He seized her hand and strained her to him once. "Meet me once more tonight," he begged, "Once more, while she sleeps—at the west gate."

It was midnight before the slow breathing of the exhausted woman told Agnes that for a few short hours she might rest beside her. Instead she stole away—softer footed than a fog wreath—and crept out to the great lodge gate where her lover waited yet her final word.

There was a fearful storm raging, but Agnes was too worn by storms within to mind the wind that wrenched the tree—tops and laid flat the dripping grass, the sheets of hammering rain, or the recurrent roar and flash the filled the heavens.

Strong arms were around her and drew her into shelter when she reached the gate. She stood panting, and looked at him in the intermittent light.

"It is the last time Robert," said she, quietly. I cannot disobey my mother. She is firm and my duty is with her. Seek another wife, my strong, true friend—one who will bring you joy, not sorrow. While my other lives and the tower stands I cannot come."

A fearful glare poured out across the sky. Every wet leaf stood out pale green and vivid, and the driving rain was lit as it rushed down. And down.

A crash that stunned them followed on the instant—a

crash that echoed from the earth to heaven and was followed by another roar, less loud but doubly awful. Before their eyes the tall tower bent and tottered, rent from turret to foundation by the stroke, and burying as it fell the ruined home and ruined life beneath it.

Strong in her pride she lived, and she died as she would have wished — by the power of the house of Clifford.

Robert bore Agnes, fainting to his sister's arms, and a newer, brighter life unfolded for the fair young girl in the bright home that now became her own.

Why I Wrote "The Yellow Wall Paper"

Many and many a reader has asked that. When the story first came out, in the *New England Magazine* about 1891, a Boston physician made protest in *The Transcript*. Such a story ought not to be written, he said; it was enough to drive anyone mad to read it.

Another physician, in Kansas I think, wrote to say that it was the best description of incipient insanity he had ever seen, and--begging my pardon--had I been there?

Now the story of the story is this:

For many years I suffered from a severe and continuous nervous breakdown tending to melancholia—and beyond. During about the third year of this trouble I went, in devout faith and some faint stir of hope, to a noted specialist in nervous diseases, the best known in the country. This wise man put me to bed and applied the rest cure, to which a still-good physique responded so promptly that he concluded there was nothing much the matter with me, and sent me home with solemn advice to "live as domestic a life as far as possible," to "have but two hours' intellectual life a day," and "never to touch pen, brush, or pencil again" as long as I lived. This was in 1887.

I went home and obeyed those directions for some three months, and came so near the borderline of utter mental ruin that I could see over.

Then, using the remnants of intelligence that remained,

and helped by a wise friend, I cast the noted specialist's advice to the winds and went to work again--work, the normal life of every human being; work, in which is joy and growth and service, without which one is a pauper and a parasite--ultimately recovering some measure of power.

Being naturally moved to rejoicing by this narrow escape, I wrote *The Yellow Wallpaper*, with its embellishments and additions, to carry out the ideal (I never had hallucinations or objections to my mural decorations) and sent a copy to the physician who so nearly drove me mad. He never acknowledged it.

The little book is valued by alienists and as a good specimen of one kind of literature. It has, to my knowledge, saved one woman from a similar fate--so terrifying her family that they let her out into normal activity and she recovered.

But the best result is this. Many years later I was told that the great specialist had admitted to friends of his that he had altered his treatment of neurasthenia since reading *The Yellow Wallpaper*.

It was not intended to drive people crazy, but to save people from being driven crazy, and it worked.

(1913) From The Forerunner

Eternal Me

What an exceeding rest 'twill be
When I can leave off being Me!
To think of it! –at last be rid
Of all the things I ever did!

Done with the varying distress
Of retroactive consciousness!
Set free to feel the joy unknown
Of Life and Love beyond my own!

Why should I long to have John Smith
Eternally to struggle with?
I'm John—but somehow cherubim
Seem quite incongruous with him.

It would not seem so queer to dwell
Eternally John Smith in Hell.
To be one man forever seems
Most fit in purgatorial dreams.

But Heaven! Rest and Power and Peace
Must surely mean the soul's release
From this small labeled entity—
This passing limitation—Me!

Water-Lure

We who were born of water, in the warm slow ancient
years,
Love it to-day for all we pay
Of terror and loss and tears.

The child laughs loud at the fountain, laughs low in the
April rain,
And the sea's bright brim is a lure to him
Where a lost life lives again.

Locked Inside

She beats upon her bolted door,
With faint weak hands;
Drearily walks the narrow floor;
Sullenly sits, blank walls before;
Despairing stands.

Life calls her, Duty, Pleasure, Gain--
Her dreams respond;
But the blank daylights wax and wane,
Dull peace, sharp agony, slow pain--
No hope beyond.

Till she comes a thought! She lifts her head,
The world grows wide!
A voice--as if clear words were said--
"Your door, o long imprisoned,
Is locked inside!"

Through This

The dawn colors creep up my bedroom wall, softly, slowly.

Darkness, a dim gray, dull blue, soft lavender, clear pink, pale yellow warm gold—sunlight.

A new day.

With the great sunrise great thoughts come.

I rise with the world. I live, I can help. Here close at hand lie the sweet home duties through which my life shall touch the others! Through this man made happier and stronger by my living; through these rosy babies sleeping here in the growing light; through this small, sweet, well-ordered home, whose restful influence shall touch all comers; through me too, perhaps—there's the baker, I must get up, or this bright purpose fades.

How well the fire burns! Its swift kindling and gathering roar speak of accomplishment. The rich odor of coffee steals through the house.

John likes morning-glories on the breakfast table—scented flowers are better with lighter meals. All is ready—healthful, dainty, delicious.

The clean-aproned little ones smile milky-mouthed over their bowls of mush. John kisses me good-bye so happily.

Through this dear work, well done, I shall reach, I shall help—but I must get the dishes done and not dream.

'Good morning! Soap, please, the same kind. Coffee, rice, two boxes of gelatine. That's all, I think. Oh—crackers! Good morning.'

There, I forgot the eggs! I can make these go, I guess.

Now to soak the tapioca. Now the beets on, they take so long. I'll bake the potatoes—they don't go in yet. Now babykins must have their bath and nap.

A clean hour and a half before dinner. I can get those little nightgowns cut and basted. How bright the sun is! Amaranth lies on the grass under the rosebush, stretching her paws among the warm, green blades. The kittens tumble over her. She's brought them three mice this week. Baby and Jack are on the warm grass too—happy, safe, well. Careful, dear! Don't go away from the little sister!

By and by when they are grown, I can—O there! the bell!

Ah, well!—yes—I'd like to have joined. I believe in it, but I can't now. Home duties forbid. This is my work. Through this, in time—there's the bell again, and it waked the baby!

As if I could buy a sewing machine every week! I'll put out a bulletin, stating my needs for the benefit of agents. I don't believe in buying at the door anyway, yet I suppose they must live. Yes, dear! Mamma's coming.

I wonder if torchon would look better, or Hamburg? It's softer but it looks older. Oh, here's that knit edging grandma sent me. Bless her dear heart!

There! I meant to have swept the bed-room this morning so as to have more time to-morrow. Perhaps I can before dinner. It does look dreadfully. I'll just put the potatoes in. Baked potatoes are so good! I love to see Jack dig into them with his little spoon.

John says I cook steak better than anyone he ever saw.

Yes, dear?

Is that so? Why, I should think they'd *know* better. Can't the people do anything about it?

Why no—not *personally*—but I should think you might. What are men for if they can't keep the city in order.

Cream on the pudding, dear?

That was a good dinner. I like to cook. I think

housework is noble if you do it in the right spirit.

That pipe must be seen to before long. I'll speak to John about it. Coal's pretty low, too.

Guess I'll put on my best boots, I want to run down town for a few moments — in case mother comes and can stay with the baby. I wonder if mother wouldn't like to join that — she has time enough. But she doesn't seem a bit interested in outside things. I ought to take baby out in her carriage, but it's so heavy with Jack, and yet Jack can't walk a great way. Besides, if mother comes I needn't. Maybe we'll all go in the car — but that's such an undertaking! Three o'clock!

Jack! Jack! Don't do that — here — wait a moment.

I ought to answer Jennie's letter. She writes such splendid things, but I don't go with her in the half she says. A woman cannot do that way and keep a family going. I'll write to her this evening.

Of course, if one could, I'd like as well as anyone to be in those great live currents of thought and action. Jennie and I were full of it in school. How long ago that seems. But I never thought then of being so happy. Jennie isn't happy, I know — she can't be, poor thing, till she's a wife and mother.

O, there comes mother! Jack, deary, open the gate for Grandma! So glad you could come, mother dear! Can you stay awhile and let me go down town on a few errands?

Mother looks real tired. I wish she would go out more and have some outside interests. Mary and the children are too much for her, I think. Harry ought not to have brought them home. Mother needs rest. She's brought up one family.

There, I've forgotten my list, I hurried so. Thread, elastic, buttons; what was that other thing? Maybe I'll think of it. How awfully cheap! How can they make them at that price! Three, please. I guess with these I can make the others last through the year. They're so pretty, too. How much are these? Jack's got to have a new coat before long — not to-day.

There, I've forgotten my list, I hurried so. Thread, elastic, buttons; what was that other thing? Maybe I'll think of it. How awfully cheap! How can they make them at that price! Three, please. I guess with these I can make the others last through the year. They're so pretty, too. How much are these? Jack's got to have a new coat before long—not to-day.

O, dear! I've missed that car, and mother can't stay after five! I'll cut across and hurry.

Why, the milk hasn't come, and John's got to go out early to-night. I wish election was over.

I'm sorry, dear, but the milk was so late I couldn't make it. Yes, I'll speak to him. O, no, I guess not; he's a very reliable man, usually, and the milk's good. Hush, hush, baby! Papa's talking!

Good night, dear, don't be late.

> Sleep, baby, sleep!
> The large stars are the sheep,
> The little stars are the lambs, I guess,
> And the fair moon is the shepherdess.
> Sleep, baby, sleep!

How pretty they look. Thank God, they keep so well.

It's not use, I can't write a letter to-night—especially to Jennie. I'm too tired. I'll go to bed early. John hates to have me wait up for him late. I'll go now, if it is before dark— then get up early tomorrow and get the sweeping done. How loud the crickets are! The evening shades creep down my bedroom wall—softly—slowly.

Warm gold—pale yellow—clear pink—soft lavender— dull blue—dim gray—darkness.

The Great Wistaria

"Meddle not with my new vine, child! See! Thou hast already broken the tender shoot! Never needle or distaff for thee, and yet thou wilt not be quiet!"

The nervous fingers wavered, clutched at a small carnelian cross that hung from her neck, then fell despairingly.

"Give me my child, mother, and then I will be quiet!"

"Hush! hush! thou fool--some one might be near! See-- there is thy father coming, even now! Get in quickly!"

She raised her eyes to her mother's face, weary eyes that yet had a flickering, uncertain blaze in their shaded depths.

"Art thou a mother and hast no pity on me, a mother? Give me my child!"

Her voice rose in a strange, low cry, broken by her father's hand upon her mouth.

"Shameless!" said he, with set teeth. "Get to thy chamber, and be not seen again to-night, or I will have thee bound!"

She went at that, and a hard-faced serving woman followed, and presently returned, bringing a key to her mistress.

"Is all well with her,--and the child also?"

"She is quiet, Mistress Dwining, well for the night, be sure. The child fretteth endlessly, but save for that it thriveth with me."

The parents were left alone together on the high square porch with its great pillars, and the rising moon began to make faint shadows of the young vine leaves that shot up luxuriantly around them; moving shadows, like little stretching fingers, on the broad and heavy planks of the oaken floor.

"It groweth well, this vine thou broughtest me in the ship, my husband."

"Aye," he broke in bitterly, "and so doth the shame I brought thee! Had I known of it I would sooner have had the ship founder beneath us, and have seen our child cleanly drowned, than live to this end!"

"Thou art very hard, Samuel, art thou not afeard for her life? She grieveth sore for the child, aye, and for the green fields to walk in!"

"Nay," said he grimly, "I fear not. She hath lost already what is more than life; and she shall have air enough soon. To-morrow the ship is ready, and we return to England. None knoweth of our stain here, not one, and if the town hath a child unaccounted for to rear in decent ways--why, it is not the first, even here. It will be well
enough cared for! And truly we have matter for thankfulness, that her cousin is yet willing to marry her."

"Hast thou told him?"

"Aye! Thinkest thou I would cast shame into another man's house, unknowing it? He hath always desired her, but she would none of him, the stubborn! She hath small choice now!"

"Will he be kind, Samuel? Can he--"

"Kind? What call'st thou it to take such as she to wife? Kind! How many men would take her, an' she had double the fortune? And being of the family already, he is glad to hide the blot forever."

"An' if she would not? He is but a coarse fellow, and she ever shunned him."

"Art thou mad, woman? She weddeth him ere we sail to-morrow, or she stayeth ever in that chamber. The girl is not so sheer a fool! He maketh an honest woman of her, and saveth our house from open shame. What other hope for her than a new life to cover the old? Let her have an honest child, an' she so longeth for one!"

He strode heavily across the porch, till the loose planks creaked again, strode back and forth, with his arms folded and his brows fiercely knit above his iron mouth.

Overhead the shadows flickered mockingly across a white face among the leaves, with eyes of wasted fire.

~

"O, George, what a house! What a lovely house! I am sure it's haunted! Let us get that house to live in this summer! We will have Kate and Jack and Susy and Jim of course, and a splendid time of it!"

Young husbands are indulgent, but still they have to recognize facts.

"My dear, the house may not be to rent; and it may also not be habitable."

"There is surely somebody in it. I am going to inquire!"

The great central gate was rusted off its hinges, and the long drive had trees in it, but a little footpath showed signs of steady usage, and up that Mrs. Jenny went, followed by her obedient George. The front windows of the old mansion were blank, but in a wing at the back they found white curtains and open doors. Outside, in the clear May sunshine, a woman was washing. She was polite and friendly, and evidently glad of visitors in that lonely place. She "guessed it could be rented--didn't know." The heirs were in Europe, but "there was a lawyer in New York had the lettin' of it." There had been folks there years ago, but not in her time. She and her husband had the rent of their part for taking care of the place. Not that they took much care on't either, "but keepin' robbers out." It was furnished throughout, old-fashioned enough, but good; and "if they took it she could do the work for 'em herself, she guessed--if *he* was willin'!"

Never was a crazy scheme more easily arranged. George knew that lawyer in New York; the rent was not alarming; and the nearness to a rising sea-shore resort made it a still pleasanter place to spend the summer.

Kate and Jack and Susy and Jim cheerfully accepted, and the June moon found them all sitting on the high front porch.

They had explored the house from top to bottom, from the great room in the garret, with nothing in it but a rickety cradle, to the well in the cellar without a curb and with a rusty chain going down to unknown blackness below. They had explored the grounds, once beautiful with rare trees and shrubs, but now a gloomy wilderness of tangled shade.

The old lilacs and laburnums, the spirea and syringa, nodded against the second-story windows. What garden plants survived were great ragged bushes or great shapeless beds. A huge wistaria vine covered the whole front of the house. The trunk, it was too large to call a stem, rose at the corner of the porch by the high steps, and had once climbed its pillars; but now the pillars were wrenched from their places and held rigid and helpless by the tightly wound and knotted arms.

It fenced in all the upper story of the porch with a knitted wall of stem and leaf; it ran along the eaves, holding up the gutter that had once supported it; it shaded every window with heavy green; and the drooping, fragrant blossoms made a waving sheet of purple from roof to ground.

"Did you ever see such a wistaria!" cried ecstatic Mrs. Jenny. "It is worth the rent just to sit under such a vine,--a fig tree beside it would be sheer superfluity and wicked extravagance!"

"Jenny makes much of her wistaria," said George, "because she's so disappointed about the ghosts. She made up her mind at first sight to have ghosts in the house, and she can't find even a ghost story!"

"No," Jenny assented mournfully; "I pumped poor Mrs. Pepperill for three days, but could get nothing out of her. But I'm convinced there is a story, if we could only find it. You need not tell me that a house like this, with a garden like this, and a cellar like this, isn't haunted!"

"I agree with you," said Jack. Jack was a reporter on a New York daily, and engaged to Mrs. Jenny's pretty sister. "And if we don't find a real ghost, you may be very sure I shall make one. It's too good an opportunity to lose!"

The pretty sister, who sat next him, resented. "You shan't do anything of the sort, Jack! This is a *real* ghostly place, and I won't have you make fun of it! Look at that group of trees out there in the long grass--it looks for all the world like a crouching, hunted figure!"

"It looks to me like a woman picking huckleberries," said Jim, who was married to George's pretty sister.

"Be still, Jim!" said that fair young woman. "I believe in Jenny's ghost as much as she does. Such a place!

Just look at this great wistaria trunk crawling up by the steps here! It looks for all the world like a writhing body--cringing--beseeching!"

"Yes," answered the subdued Jim, "it does, Susy. See its waist,--about two yards of it, and twisted at that! A waste of good material!"

"Don't be so horrid, boys! Go off and smoke somewhere if you can't be congenial!"

"We can! We will! We'll be as ghostly as you please." And forthwith they began to see bloodstains and crouching figures so plentifully that the most delightful shivers multiplied, and the fair enthusiasts started for bed, declaring they should never sleep a wink.

"We shall all surely dream," cried Mrs. Jenny, "and we must all tell our dreams in the morning!"

"There's another thing certain," said George, catching

Susy as she tripped over a loose plank; "and that is that you frisky creatures must use the side door till I get this Eiffel tower of a portico fixed, or we shall have some fresh ghosts on our hands! We found a plank here that yawns like a trap-door--big enough to swallow you,--and I believe the bottom of the thing is in China!"

The next morning found them all alive, and eating a substantial New England breakfast, to the accompaniment of saws and hammers on the porch, where carpenters of quite miraculous promptness were tearing things to pieces generally.

"It's got to come down mostly," they had said. "These timbers are clean rotted through, what ain't pulled out o' line by this great creeper. That's about all that holds the thing up."

There was clear reason in what they said, and with a caution from anxious Mrs. Jenny not to hurt the wistaria, they were left to demolish and repair at leisure.

"How about ghosts?" asked Jack after a fourth griddle cake. "I had one, and it's taken away my appetite!"

Mrs. Jenny gave a little shriek and dropped her knife and fork.

"Oh, so had I! I had the most awful--well, not dream exactly, but feeling. I had forgotten all about it!"

"Must have been awful," said Jack, taking another cake. "Do tell us about the feeling. My ghost will wait."

"It makes me creep to think of it even now," she said. "I woke up, all at once, with that dreadful feeling as if something were going to happen, you know! I was wide awake, and hearing every little sound for miles around, it seemed to me. There are so many strange little noises in the country for all it is so still. Millions of crickets and things outside, and all kinds of rustles in the trees! There wasn't much wind, and the moonlight came through in my three great windows in three white squares on the black old floor, and those fingery wistaria leaves we were talking of last night just seemed to crawl all over them. And--O, girls, you know that dreadful well in the cellar?"

A most gratifying impression was made by this, and Jenny proceeded cheerfully:

"Well, while it was so horridly still, and I lay there trying not to wake George, I heard as plainly as if it were right in the room, that old chain down there rattle and creak over the stones!"

"Bravo!" cried Jack. "That's fine! I'll put it in the Sunday edition!"

"Be still!" said Kate. "What was it, Jenny? Did you really see anything?"

"No, I didn't, I'm sorry to say. But just then I didn't want to. I woke George, and made such a fuss that he gave me bromide, and said he'd go and look, and that's the last I thought of it till Jack reminded me,--the bromide worked so well."

"Now, Jack, give us yours," said Jim. "Maybe, it will dovetail in somehow. Thirsty ghost, I imagine; maybe they had prohibition here even then!"

Jack folded his napkin, and leaned back in his most impressive manner.

"It was striking twelve by the great hall clock--" he began.

"There isn't any hall clock!"

"O hush, Jim, you spoil the current! It was just one o'clock then, by my old-fashioned repeater."

"Waterbury! Never mind what time it was!"

"Well, honestly, I woke up sharp, like our beloved hostess, and tried to go to sleep again, but couldn't. I experienced all those moonlight and grasshopper sensations, just like Jenny, and was wondering what could have been the matter with the supper, when in came my ghost, and I knew it was all a dream! It was a female ghost, and I imagine she was young and handsome, but all those crouching, hunted figures of last evening ran riot in my brain, and this poor creature looked just like them. She was all wrapped up in a shawl, and had a big bundle under her arm,--dear me, I am spoiling the story! With the air and gait of one in frantic haste and terror, the muffled figure glided to a dark old bureau, and seemed taking things from the drawers. As she turned, the moonlight shone full on a little red cross that hung from her neck by a thin gold chain--I saw it glitter as she crept

noiselessly from the room! That's all."

"O Jack, don't be so horrid! Did you really? Is that all? What do you think it was?"

"I am not horrid by nature, only professionally. I really did. That was all. And I am fully convinced it was the genuine, legitimate ghost of an eloping chambermaid with kleptomania!"

"You are too bad, Jack!" cried Jenny. "You take all the horror out of it. There isn't a 'creep' left among us."

"It's no time for creeps at nine-thirty A.M., with sunlight and carpenters outside!

However, if you can't wait till twilight for your creeps, I think I can furnish one or two," said George. "I went down cellar after Jenny's ghost!"

There was a delighted chorus of female voices, and Jenny cast upon her lord a glance of genuine gratitude.

"It's all very well to lie in bed and see ghosts, or hear them," he went on. "But the young householder suspecteth burglars, even though as a medical man he knoweth nerves, and after Jenny dropped off I started on a voyage of discovery. I never will again, I promise you!"

"Why, what *was* it?"

"Oh, George!"

"I got a candle--"

"Good mark for the burglars," murmured Jack.

"And went all over the house, gradually working down to the cellar and the well."

"Well?" said Jack.

"Now you can laugh; but that cellar is no joke by daylight, and a candle there at night is about as inspiring as a lightning-bug in the Mammoth Cave. I went along with the light, trying not to fall into the well prematurely; got to it all at once; held the light down and *then* I saw, right under my feet--(I nearly fell over her, or walked through her, perhaps),--a woman, hunched up under a shawl! She had hold of the chain, and the candle shone on her hands--white, thin hands,--on a little red cross that hung from her neck--*vide* Jack! I'm no believer in ghosts, and I firmly object to unknown parties in the house at night; so I spoke to her rather fiercely. She didn't seem to notice that, and I reached down to take hold of her,--then I came upstairs!"

"What for?"

"What happened?"

"What was the matter?"

"Well, nothing happened. Only she wasn't there! May have been indigestion, of course, but as a physician I don't advise any one to court indigestion alone at midnight in a cellar!"

"This is the most interesting and peripatetic and evasive ghost I ever heard of!" said Jack. "It's my belief she has no end of silver tankards, and jewels galore, at the bottom of that well, and I move we go and see!"

"To the bottom of the well, Jack?"

"To the bottom of the mystery. Come on!"

There was unanimous assent, and the fresh cambrics and pretty boots were gallantly escorted below by gentlemen whose jokes were so frequent that many of them were a little forced.

The deep old cellar was so dark that they had to bring lights, and the well so gloomy in its blackness that the ladies recoiled.

"That well is enough to scare even a ghost. It's my opinion you'd better let well enough alone!" quoth Jim.

"Truth lies hid in a well, and we must get her out," said George. "Bear a hand with the chain?"

Jim pulled away on the chain, George turned the creaking windlass, and Jack was chorus.

"A wet sheet for this ghost, if not a flowing sea," said he. "Seems to be hard work raising spirits! I suppose he kicked the bucket when he went down!"

As the chain lightened and shortened there grew a strained silence among them; and when at length the bucket appeared, rising slowly through the dark water, there was an eager, half reluctant peering, and a natural drawing back. They poked the gloomy contents. "Only water."

"Nothing but mud."

"Something--"

They emptied the bucket up on the dark earth, and then the girls all went out into the air, into the bright warm sunshine in front of the house, where was the sound of saw and hammer, and the smell of new wood. There was nothing said until the men joined them, and then Jenny timidly asked:

"How old should you think it was, George?"

"All of a century," he answered. "That water is a preservative,--lime in it. Oh!--you mean?--Not more than a month; a very little baby!"

There was another silence at this, broken by a cry from the workmen. They had removed the floor and the side walls of the old porch, so that the sunshine poured down to the dark stones of the cellar bottom. And there, in the strangling grasp of the roots of the great wistaria, lay the bones of a woman, from whose neck still hung a tiny scarlet cross on a thin chain of gold.

The Room at the Top

There is room at the top?
Ah yes! Were you ever there?
Do you know what they bear
Whose struggle does not stop
Till they reach the room at the top?

Think you first of the way,
How long from the bottom round,--
From the safe, warm, common ground
In the light of the common day--
'Tis a long way. A dark way.

And think of the fight.
It is not so hard to stand
And strive off the broad free land;
But to climb in the wind and night,
And fight,--and climb,--and fight!

And the top when you enter in!
Ah! the fog! The frost! The dark!
And the hateful voices--hark!
O the comfort that you win!
Yes, there's room at the top. Come in!

The Rocking Chair

A waving spot of sunshine, a signal light that caught the eye at once in a waste of commonplace houses, and all the dreary dimness of a narrow city street.

Across some low roof that made a gap in the wall of masonry, shot a level, brilliant beam of the just-setting sun, touching the golden head of a girl in an open window.

She sat in a high-backed rocking-chair with brass mountings that glittered as it swung, rocking slowly back and forth, never lifting her head, but fairly lighting up the street with the glory of her sunlit hair.

We two stopped and stared, and, so staring, caught sight of a small sign in a lower window—'Furnished Lodgings.' With a common impulse we crossed the street and knocked at the dingy front door.

Slow, even footsteps approached from within, and a soft girlish laugh ceased suddenly as the door opened, showing us an old woman, with a dull, expressionless face and faded eyes.

Yes, she had rooms to let. Yes, we could see them. No, there was no service. No, there were no meals. So murmuring monotonously, she led the way up-stairs. It was an ordinary house enough, on a poor sort of street, a house in no way remarkable or unlike its fellows.

She showed us two rooms, connected, neither better nor worse than most of their class, rooms without a striking feature about them, unless it was the great brass-bound chair we found still rocking gently by the window.

But the gold-haired girl was nowhere to be seen.

I fancied I heard the light rustle of girlish robes in the inner chamber—a breath of that low laugh—but the door leading to this apartment was locked, and when I asked the woman if we could see the other rooms she said she had no other rooms to let.

A few words aside with Hal, and we decided to take these two, and move in at once. There was no reason we should not. We were looking for lodgings when that swinging sunbeam caught our eyes, and the accommodations were fully as good as we could pay for. So we closed our bargain on the spot, returned to our deserted boarding-house for a few belongings, and were settled anew that night.

Hal and I were young newspaper men, 'penny-a-liners,' part of that struggling crowd of aspirants who are to literature what squires and pages were to knighthood in olden days. We were winning our spurs. So far it was slow work, unpleasant an dill-paid—so was squireship and pagehood, I am sure; menial service and laborious polishing of armour; long running afoot while the master rode. But the squire could at least honor his lord and leader, while we, alas! Had small honor for those above us in our profession, with but too good reason. We, of course, should do far nobler things when these same spurs were won!

Now it may have been mere literary instinct—the grasping at 'material' of the pot-boiling writers of the day, and it may have been another kind of instinct—the unacknowledged attraction of the fair unknown; but, whatever the reason, the place had drawn us both, and here we were.

Unbroken friendship begun in babyhood held us two together, all the more closely because Hal was a merry, prosaic, clear-headed fellow, and I sensitive and romantic.

The fearless frankness of family life we shared, but held the right to unapproachable reserves, and so kept love unstrained.

We examined our new quarters with interest. The front room, Hal's, was rather big and bare. The back room, mine, rather small and bare.

He preferred that room, I am convinced, because of the window and the chair. I preferred the other, because of the locked door. We neither of us mentioned these prejudices.

"Are you sure you would not rather have this room?" asked Hal, conscious, perhaps of an ulterior motive in his choice.

"No, indeed," said I, with a similar reservation; "you only have the street and I have a real 'view' from my window. The only thing I begrudge you is the chair!"

"You may come and rock therein at any hour of the day or night," said he magnanimously. "It is tremendously comfortable, for all its black looks."

It was a comfortable chair, a very comfortable chair, and we both used it a great deal. A very high-backed chair, curving a little forward at the top, with heavy square corners. These corners, the ends of the rockers, the great shape knobs that tipped the arms, and every other point and angle were mounted in brass.

"Might be used for a batter — ram!" said Hal.

He sat smoking in it, rocking slowly and complacently by the window, while I lounged on the foot of the bed, and watched a pale young moon sink slowly over the western housetops.

It went out of sight at last, and the room grew darker and darker till I could only see Hal's handsome head and the curving chair-back move slowly to and fro against the dim sky.

"What brought us here so suddenly, Maurice?" he asked, out of the dark.

"Three reasons," I answered. "Our need of lodgings, the suitability of these, and a beautiful head."

"Correct," said he. "Anything else?"

"Nothing you would admit the existence of, my sternly logical friend. But I am conscious of a certain compulsion, or at least attraction, in the case, which does not seem wholly accounted for, even by golden hair."

"For once I will agree with you," said Hal. "I feel the same way myself, and I am not impressionable."

We were silent for a little. I may have closed my eyes, and—it may have been longer than I thought, but it did not seem another moment when something brushed softly against my arm, and Hal in his great chair was rocking beside me.

"Excuse me," said he, seeing me start. "This chair evidently 'walks,' I've seen 'em before."

So had I, on carpets, but there was no carpet here, and I thought I was awake.

He pulled the heavy thing back to the window again, and we went to bed.

Our door was open, and we could talk back and forth, but presently I dropped off and slept heavily until morning. But I must have dreamed most vividly, for he accused me of rocking in his chair half the night; said he could see my outline clearly against the starlight.

"No," said I, "you dreamed it. You've got rocking-chair on the brain."

"Dream it is, then," he answered cheerily. "Better a nightmare than a contradiction; a vampire than a quarrel! Come on, let's go to breakfast!"

We wondered greatly as the days went by that we saw nothing of our golden-haired charmer. But we wondered in silence, and neither mentioned it to the other.

Sometimes I heard her light movements in the room next mine, or the soft laugh somewhere in the house; but the mother's slow, even steps were more frequent, and even she was not often visible.

All either of us saw of the girl, to my knowledge, was from the street, for she still availed herself or our chair by the window. This we disapproved of, on principle, the more so as we left the doors locked, and her presence proved the possession of another key. No; there was the door in my room! But I did not mention the idea. Under the circumstances, however, we made no complaint, and used to rush stealthily and swiftly up-stairs, hoping to surprise her. But we never succeeded. Only the chair was often found still rocking, and sometimes, I fancied a faint sweet odor lingering about , an odor strangely saddening and suggestive. But one day when I thought Hal was there I rushed in unceremoniously and caught her. It was but a glimpse—a swift, light, noiseless sweep—she vanished into my own room. Following her with apologies for such a sudden entrance, I was too late. The envious door was locked again.

Our landlady's fair daughter was evidently shy enough when brought to bay, but strangely willing to take liberties in our absence.

Still, I had seen her, and for that sight would have forgiven much. Hers was a strange beauty, infinitely attractive yet infinitely perplexing. I marveled in secret, and longed with painful eagerness for another meeting; but I said nothing to Hal of my surprising her—it did not seem fair to the girl~ She might have some good reason or going there; perhaps I could meet her again.

So I took to coming home early, on one excuse or another, and inventing all manner of errands to get to the room when Hal was not in.

But it was not until after numberless surprises on that point, finding him there when I supposed him downtown, and noticing something a little forced in his needless explanations, that I began to wonder if he might not be on the same quest.

Soon I was sure of it. I reached the corner of the street one evening just at sunset, and –yes, there was the rhythmic swing of that bright head in the dark frame of the open window. There also was Hal in the street below. She looked out, she smiled. He let himself in and went up-stairs.

I quickened my pace. I was in time to see the movement stop, the fair head turn, and Hal standing beyond her in the shadow.

I passed the door, passed the street, walked an hour—two hours—got a late supper somewhere, and came back about bedtime with a sharp and bitter feeling in my hear that I strove in vain to reason down. Why he had not as good a right to meet her as I it were hard to say, and yet I was strangely angry with him.

When I returned the lamplight shone behind the white curtain, and the shadow of the great chair stood motionless against it. Another shadow crossed—Hal—smoking. I went up.

He greeted me effusively and asked why I was so late. Where I got supper. Was unnaturally cheerful. There was a sudden dreadful sense of concealment between us. But he told nothing and I asked nothing, and we went silently to bed.

I blamed him for saying no word about our fair mystery, and yet I had said none concerning my own meeting. I racked my brain with question as to how much he had really seen of her; if she had talked to him; what she had told him; how long she had stayed.

I tossed all night and Hal was sleepless too, for I heard him rocking for hours, by the window, by the bed, close to my door. I never knew a rocking-chair to 'walk' as that one did.

Towards morning the steady creak and swing was too much for my nerves or temper.

"For goodness' sake, Hal, do stop that and go to bed!"

'What?' came a sleepy voice.

'Don't fool!' said I, 'I haven't slept a wink to-night for your everlasting rocking. Now do leave off and go to bed.'

'Go to bed! I've been in bed all night and I wish you had! Can't you use the chair without blaming me for it?'

And all the time I heard him *rock, rock, rock,* over by the hall door! I rose stealthily and entered the room, meaning to surprise the ill-timed joker and convict him in the act.

Both rooms were full of the dim phosphorescence of reflected moonlight; I knew them even in the dark; and yet I stumbled just inside the door, and fell heavily.

Hal was out of bed in a moment and had struck a light.

'Are you hurt, my dear boy?'

I was hurt, and solely by his fault, for the chair was not where I supposed, but close to my bedroom door, where he must have left it to leap into bed when he heard me coming. So it was in no amiable humor that I refused his offers of assistance and limped back to my own sleepless pillow. I had struck my ankle on one of those brass-tipped rockers, and it pained me severely. I never saw a chair so made to hurt as that one. It was so large and heavy and ill-balanced, and every joint and corner so shod with brass . Hal and I had punished ourselves enough on it before, especially in the dark when we forgot where the thing was standing, but never so severely as this. It was not like Hal to play such tricks, and both heart and ankle ached as I crept into bed again to toss and doze and dream and fitfully start till morning.

Hal was kindness itself, but he would insist that he had been asleep and I rocking all night, till I grew actually angry with him.

'That's carrying a joke too far,' I said at last. 'I don't mind a joke, even when it hurts, but there are limits.'

'Yes, there are!' said he, significantly, and we dropped the subject.

Several days passed. Hal had repeated meetings with the gold-haired damsel; this I saw from the street; but save for these bitter glimpses I waited vainly.

It was hard to bear, harder almost than the growing estrangement between Hal and me, and that cut deeply. I think that at last either one of us would have been glad to go away by himself, but neither was willing to leave the other to the room, the chair, the beautiful unknown.

Coming home one morning unexpectedly, I found the dull-faced landlady arranging the rooms, and quite laid myself out to make an impression upon her, to no purpose.

'That is a fine old chair you have there,' said I, as she stood mechanically polishing the brass corners with her apron.

She looked at the darkly glittering thing with almost a flash of pride.

'Yes,' she said, 'a fine chair!'

'Is it old!' I pursued.

'Very old,' she answered briefly.

'But I thought rocking-chairs were a modern American invention!' said I.

She looked at me apathetically.

'It is Spanish,' she said, 'Spanish oak, Spanish leather, Spanish brass, Spanish — .' I did not catch the last word, and she left the room without another.

It was a strange ill-balanced thing, that chair, though so easy and comfortable to sit in. The rockers were long and sharp behind, always lying in wait for the unwary, but cut short in front; and the back was so high and so heavy on top, that what with its weight and the shortness of the front rockers, it tipped forward with an ease and a violence equally astonishing.

This I knew from experience, as it had plunged over upon me during some of our frequent encounters. Hal also was a sufferer, but in spite of our manifold bruises, neither of us would have had the chair removed, for did not she sit in it, evening after evening, and rock there in the golden light of the setting sun.

So, evening after evening, we two fled from our work as early as possible, and hurried home alone, by separate ways, to the dingy street and the glorified window.

I could not endure forever. When Hal came home first, I, lingering in the street below, could see through our window that lovely head and his in close proximity. When I came first, it was to catch perhaps a quick glance from above—a bewildering smile—no more. She was always gone when I reached the room, and the inner door of my chamber irrevocably locked.

At times I even caught the click of the latch, heard the flutter of loose robes on the other side; and sometimes this daily disappointment, this constant agony of hope deferred, would bring me to my knees by that door, begging her to open to me, crying to her in every term of passionate endearment and persuasion that tortured heart of man could think to use.

Hal had neither word nor look for me now, save those of studied politeness and cold indifference, and how could I behave otherwise to him, so proven to my face a liar?

I saw him from the street one night, in the broad level sunlight, sitting in that chair, with the beautiful head on his shoulder. It as more than I could bear. If he had won, and won so utterly, I would ask but to speak to her once, and say farewell to both for ever. So I heavily climbed the stairs, knocked loudly, and entered at Hal's 'Come in!' only to find him sitting there alone, smoking—yes, smoking in the chair which but a moment since had held her too!

He had but just lit the cigar, a paltry device to blind my eyes.

'Look here, Hal,' said I, 'I can't stand this any longer. May I ask you one thing? Let me see her once, just once, that

I may say good-bye, and then neither of you need see me again!'

Hal rose to his feet and looked me straight in the eye. Then he threw that whole cigar out of the window, and walked to within two feet of me.

'Are you crazy,' he said, 'I ask her! I have never had speech of her in my life! And you—' He stopped and turned away.

'And I what?' I would have it out now whatever came.

'And you have seen her day after day—talked with her—I need not repeat all that my eyes have seen!'

'You need not, indeed,' said I. 'It would tax even your invention. I have never seen her in this room but once, and then but for a fleeting glimpse—no word. From the street I have seen her often—with you!'

He turned very white and walked from me to the window then turned again.

'I have never seen her in this room for even such a moment as you own to. From the street I have seen her often—*with you!*'

We looked at each other.

'Do you mean to say,' I inquired slowly, 'that I did not see you just now sitting in that chair, by that window, with her in your arms?'

'Stop!' he cried, throwing out his hand with a fierce gesture. It struck sharply on the corner of the chair-back. He wiped the blood mechanically from the three-cornered cut, looking fixedly at me.

'I saw you,' said I.

'You did not!' said he.

I turned slowly on my heel and went into my room. I could not bear to tell that man, my more than brother, that he lied.

I sat down on my bed with my head on my hands, and presently I heard Hal's door open and shut, his step on the stair, the front door slam behind him. He had gone, I knew not where, and if he went to his death and a word of mine would have stopped him, I would not have said it. I do not know how long I sat there, in the company of hopeless love and jealousy and hate.

Suddenly, out of the silence of the empty room, came the steady swing and creak of the great chair. Perhaps—it must be! I sprang to my feet and noiselessly opened the door. There she sat by the window, looking out, and—yes—she threw a kiss to some one below. Ah, how beautiful she was! How beautiful! I made a step toward her. I held out my hands, I uttered I know not what—when all at once came Hal's quick step upon the stairs.

She heard it, too, giving me one look, one subtle, mysterious, triumphant look, slipped past me and into my room just as Hal burst in. He saw her go. He came straight to me and I thought he would have struck me down where I stood.

'Out of my way,' he cried. 'I will speak to her. Is it not enough to see?'—he motioned toward the window with his wounded hand—'Let me pass!'

'She is not there,' I answered. 'She has gone through into the other room.'

A light laugh sounded close by us, a faint, soft, silver laugh, almost at my elbow.

He flung me from his path, threw open the door, and entered. The room was empty.

'Where have you hidden her?' he demanded. I coldly pointed to the other door.

'So her room opens into yours, does it?' he muttered with a bitter smile. 'No wonder you preferred the "view"! Perhaps I can open it too?' And he laid his hands upon the latch.

I smiled then, for bitter experience had taught me that it was always locked, locked to all my prayers and entreaties.

Let him kneel there as I had! But it opened under his hand! I sprang to his side, and we looked into—a closet, two by four, as bare and shallow as an empty coffin!

He turned to me, as white with rage as I was with terror. I was not thinking of him.

'What have you done with her?' he cried. And then contemptuously—'That I should stop to question a liar!'

I paid no heed to him, but walked back into the other room, where the great chair rocked by the window.

He followed me, furious with disappointment, and laid his hand upon the swaying back, his strong fingers closing on it till the nails were white.

'Will you leave this place?' said he.

'No,' said I.

'I will live no longer with a liar and traitor,' said he.

'Then you will have to kill yourself,' said I.

With a muttered oath he sprang upon me, but caught his foot in the long rocker, and fell heavily.

So wild a wave of hate rose in my heart that I could have trampled upon him where he lay—killed him like a dog—but with a mighty effort I turned from him and left the room.

When I returned it was broad day. Early and still, not sunrise yet, but full of hard, clear light on roof and wall and roadway. I stopped on the lower floor to find the landlady and announce my immediate departure. Door after door I knocked at, tried and opened; room after room I entered and searched thoroughly; in all that house, from cellar to garret, was no furnished room but ours, no sign of human occupancy. Dust, dust, and cobwebs everywhere. Nothing else.

With a strange sinking of the heart I came back to our own door.

Surely I heard the landlady's slow, even step inside, and that soft, low laugh. I rushed in.

The room was empty of all life; both rooms utterly empty.

Yes, of all life; for, with the love of a lifetime surging in my heart, I sprang to where Hal lay beneath the window, and found him dead.

Dead, and most horribly dead. Three heavy marks — blows — three deep, three-cornered gashes — I started to my feet — even the chair had gone!

Again the whispered laugh. Out of that house of terror I fled desperately.

From the street I cast one shuddering glance at the fateful window.

The risen sun was gilding all the housetops, and its level rays, striking the high panes on the building opposite, shone back in a calm glory on the great chair by the window, the sweet face, down-dropped eyes, and swaying golden head.

The Sands

It runs--it runs--the hourglass turning;
Dark sands glooming, bright sands burning;
I turn--and turn--with heavy or hopeful hands;
So must I turn as long as the Voice commands;
But I lose all count of the hours for watching the sliding
sands.

Or fast--or slow--it ceases turning;
Ceases the flow, or bright or burning--
"What have you done with the hours?" the Voice demands.
What can I say of eager or careless hands?--
I had forgotten the hours in watching the sliding sands.

For Fear

For fear of prowling beasts at night
They blocked the cave;
Women and children hid from sight,
Men scarce more brave.

For fear of warrior's sword and spear
They barred the gate;
Women and children lived in fear,
Men lived in hate.

For fear of criminals to-day
We lock the door;
Women and children still to stay
Hid evermore.

Come out! You need no longer hide!
What fear ye now?
No wolf nor lion waits outside--
Only a cow.

Come out! The world approaches peace,
War nears its end;
No warrior watches your release--
Only a friend.

Come out! The night of crime his fled--
Day is begun;
Here is no criminal to dread--
Only your son!

The world, half yours, demands your care,
Waken, and come!
Make it a woman's world, safe, fair,
Garden and home!

THE YELLOW WALLPAPER
Adapted by Aric Cushing and Logan Thomas
(Excerpt)

CREDITS ROLL OVER:

The blighted, desolate plains of the American West.

The giant red sun rises over the horizon, filling the frame with fire.

The year is 1892.

                                    CUT TO:

EXT. MOUNTAIN GROVE. DAY.

People move through the charred remains of houses. Chimneys still stand, strange pillars of brick amidst the blackened, scorched wood.

An OLD WOMAN pokes through the remains with a stick.

A man, JOHN WEILAND, stands and stares at the smoldering fire. His face hangs from shock, black smudges spackle his face.

John Weiland is a thirty five year old physician, of wise features, with small spectacles, brown receding hair and a medium frame.

Behind him, bodies move like ghosts.

A woman wanders through the evidence of her destroyed house, weeping.

John surveys the destruction.

                                        CUT TO:

ONE WEEK LATER.

EXT. DIRT ROAD. DAY.

A carriage rumbles over the dirt road.

JENNIE GASKELL, sister to CHARLOTTE WEILAND, sits in the back seat. She holds her sister's face in her chest, as Charlotte weeps uncontrollably. Both women are turned away, their faces hidden.

John sits in the carriage with the women. He stares out the window, disengaged.

                                        CUT TO:

EXT. DIRT ROAD. DAY.

Mist crawls low as the trees hang heavily.
A black carriage moves under a canopy of
branches.

                                    CUT TO:

EXT. THE WAKEFIELD HOUSE. DAY.

MR. HENDRICKS, bank solicitor, walks with
John around the house.

                    MR. HENDRICKS O.C.
          The house is full. You can
          add anything you like, but
          please do not take anything
          with you.

                    JOHN
          We do not have anything.

Mr. Hendricks laughs, gently. John is
nervous and exhausted.

                    MR. HENDRICKS
          Well. . . all that you may
          need has most likely been
          left behind in the house.

                    JOHN
          The house has well water?

                    MR. HENDRICKS
          Yes. Of course.

                    JOHN
          Have you worked for the
          Wakefields very long, Mr.
          Hendricks?

                    MR. HENDRICKS
          Isaac.

                    JOHN
          Isaac.

                    MR. HENDRICKS
          Oh yes. It is always difficult.
          . . finding the right people.
          But I can tell that you are
          different. Good folk...

                    JOHN
          Thank you.

                    MR. HENDRICKS
          The great expanse of land you
          saw on the way here. . . you
          can use that as a short cut back
          to town.(beat) It will be about
          twenty five minutes. Walking, that
          is.

                    JOHN
                    (nods)
          I can only pay you for two months--
          to start.

                    MR. HENDRICKS
          One is fine. (beat) Oh yes. I would
          not try to grow anything. The ground
          is dead.

                                        CUT TO:

Jennie and Charlotte sit in the carriage
in the distance.

SHOT THROUGH THE GLASS OF THE HORSE
CARRIAGE:

CHARLOTTE WEILAND sits in the passenger seat. Her jet black hair is bundled up on her head, as is the fashion of the time, and her soot-covered dress folds about her. Her face is stark and angular. She is mid to late thirties.

                    JENNIE O.C.
          It's larger than I thought.

Charlotte opens the door and steps out of the carriage.

Jennie Gaskell follows her sister. Jennie is 44 and extremely thin. She has tough, angular features and a wizened face.

Jennie reaches down and sifts her hand through the dirt. She examines it for richness.

                                        CUT TO:

CLOSE UP

of Charlotte as she turns towards the house. She has a strange beauty, with a long thin neck and delicate features.

CUT TO:

EXT. FRONT PORCH. DAY.

John turns the corner with Mr. Hendricks.

                    MR. HENDRICKS
          Well.

Mr. Hendricks fishes into his pocket and pulls out a key.

                    MR. HENDRICKS (CONT'D)
          Here you are.

                         JOHN
          Oh. Yes.

Jennie and Charlotte stand back on the
porch, the house looming behind them.

                    MR. HENDRICKS
                    (looking out)
          It's all done then.

Long silence.

                    MR. HENDRICKS
                    (tipping)
          Ladies.

John, Charlotte and Jennie watch as Mr.
Hendricks turns and walks away.

                                   CUT TO:

INT. ENTRYWAY. DAY.

WE MOVE INTO THE house with John, Jennie
and Charlotte.

Dust sparkles in the rays of sunlight
falling through the tall windows. It is a
cavernous entrance. The foyer is large,
with massive wooden doors that slide shut
on all sides. The walls are covered with
paintings and tapestries, all one upon
another.

John, Charlotte, and Jennie stand dwarfed
in the expanse.

                    JOHN
          Well.

                    JENNIE
          What first?

                    CHARLOTTE
          I think a bedroom. I need to
          lie down.

                                        CUT TO:

INT. FIRST HALLWAY. DAY.

John, Charlotte and Jennie's shoes clunk
over the wood floor.

John opens the door to a room.

They step inside.

                                        CUT TO:

INT. JENNIE'S ROOM. DAY.

Jennie runs her hand along the blanket of
the bed.

The room is simple and conservative--drab.
A chest of drawers against the wall, a
single bed, a standing closet.

John and Charlotte stand in the doorway as
Jennie goes to the closet.

                    JENNIE
          It looks like the maid's quarters.
          Charlotte turns and exits the room.

                    JOHN
          If you don't like it, this is
          perfectly... (John watches Charlotte
          exit) fine for us. We can take it.
          . .

                    JENNIE
          No. I didn't mean that.

                                        CUT TO:

INT. LIBRARY. DAY.

The stuck door groans then CRACKS open.
John and Jennie move inside.

The library is revealed in a shocking
display of brooding shadow and mahogany.
The walls are stacked with dusty books and
animal heads.

                                        CUT TO:

INT. JOHN AND CHARLOTTE'S ROOM. DAY.

Charlotte moves into the main bedroom. She
crosses the deep gold carpet and
sits on the bed.

WE PULL IN

to her from behind as she reaches for
something in her pocket. She pulls out
tiny, crumpled pieces of paper, covered
with writing. She looks down to the
fragile pages.

                                        CUT TO:

INT. LIBRARY. DAY.

Jennie sits on the sofa. A large fireplace looms behind her.

                    JENNIE
          There may be some flour, but I would
          be surprised if there is much of
          anything else.

                    JOHN
          I'm really not very hungry.

John looks through the books.

                    JOHN (CONT'D)
          I don't think Charlotte will want to
          eat.

                    JENNIE
               (hint of exhausted sarcasm)
          Well if Charlotte's not hungry, you
          are not hungry, and I am not hungry,
          I suppose there is no need to make
          dinner tonight then.

                    JOHN
               (looking at her exasperated)
          I suppose not.

                    JENNIE
          Tell me, how long did that man say
          it had been since the last people
          lived here?

                    JOHN
          He didn't. Why?

                    JENNIE
          I find it strange that the house is
          covered in dust, but the plants are
          well watered.

                    JOHN
          I suppose.

John lost in his book--

After a moment, he looks up.

John just catches a glimpse of Jennie's
head moving through the door, as the door
closes.

                              CUT TO:

John sits down on the sofa. He begins to
cry.

                              CUT TO:

INT. JOHN AND CHARLOTTE'S ROOM. NIGHT.

John undoes the suspenders and begins to
take off his shirt.

Charlotte is curled in bed, facing the
window. She stares forward.

After a moment, John gets into bed. John
lies next to her. He curls up and watches
the back of Charlotte's head.

He turns away from her, and says nothing.

                              CUT TO:

INT. FIRST HALLWAY. NIGHT.

Jennie emerges from the sewing room and closes the door. She moves down the hallway. She douses out the large oil lamps hanging from the ceiling with a metal extension.

The library door squeaks open.
An amber glow flickers from the room.

Jennie turns--

She goes to the door and slowly pushes it open.

> JENNIE
> John?

CUT TO:

INT. LIBRARY. NIGHT.

Jennie steps into the room.

HOLD ON the library.

Jennie moves through the room.

Spooked, Jennie goes to the lamp. It illuminates the centerpiece portrait of the library: a massive painting of what appears to be a Dutch merchant.

Jennie leans down and reads the brass tag name on the painting. It is too dirty to make out. Jennie rubs her finger over the tag. It reads -

'Eckhart van Wakefield'.

CUT TO:

INT. WAKEFIELD HOUSE. DINING ROOM. NEXT DAY.

CLOSE UP

Bowl of oats.

                    JENNIE
          There were oats left.

John stares down at the oats.

Jennie sits down at the table with her bowl.

Charlotte weakly picks up her spoon.

                    JENNIE
                 (passionless)
          I'm going to do a thorough cleaning
          today...to see what we have gotten
          ourselves into.

                    JOHN
          Fine. I'll go into town and see what
          they have for work.

                    JENNIE
          Do you mean patients?

                    JOHN
          Patients, labor. Whatever I can get.

                    CHARLOTTE
          John--

                    JENNIE
          It's only been little more than a
          week.

                    JOHN
          Really Jennie. How long should I
          wait?

                    CHARLOTTE
          But you.   . .are a professional,
          John. You should not take just any
          job.

                    JOHN
          Well, we should not have kept our
          money in the house. You did not want
          to put it in the bank. So. . . I
          will take whatever I can find for
          now.

Charlotte shrinks in her chair.

                    JOHN
          What little Jack loaned us will not
          get us very far.

Jennie gets up from the table angry.

                    JENNIE
          As long as you are going into town
          then, there is a list of things we
          need.

                                        CUT TO:

EXT. SIDE OF THE WAKEFIELD HOUSE. DAY.

John examines a bicycle resting against
the wall.

                                        CUT TO:

INT. DINING ROOM. DAY.

Jennie sweeps the floor.

Charlotte cleans the dining room table.

                              CUT TO:

EXT. DRY LAKE BED. DAY.

John bicycles over the dry lake bed, a
small speck against a backdrop of
mountain.

The wheels spin, giving off a metallic
buzz.

                              CUT TO:

INT. SITTING ROOM. DAY.

Jennie brushes the curtains with a duster.
Her foot kicks a large box at the base of
the window.

Jennie looks down at it.

                    JENNIE
              (to Charlotte)
          Can you help me?

They both attempt to move the box.

                    CHARLOTTE
          It's not moving at all.

                              CUT TO:

EXT. DIRT ROAD. DAY.

John turns into the forest.

A solitary road.

                                              CUT TO:

INT. SITTING ROOM. DAY.

Jennie leans down and opens the lid.
Both sisters look at the contents.

                    JENNIE
          It's dirt.

Charlotte leans down and sifts her hand
through it.

                    JENNIE (CONT'D)
          Just dirt.

Jennie leans the lid against the wall. She
kneels down and puts both hands through
it.

                    CHARLOTTE
          Why?

Jennie shakes her head in bewilderment.

                    JENNIE
          I don't know.

                                              CUT TO:

INT. FOREST GROVE. DAY.

John stops the bicycle. He's tired and
sweating. Suddenly, he spots something
around the bend of the path.

Movement.

John walks the bike towards it.

CUT TO:

JOHN POV

of the road up ahead. In the distance, a man stands on the side of the road with a wheelbarrow. John cannot make out the scene.

The noon day sun melts the air.

John squints.

Continues on.

Finally, John comes up to the man. A strange WOMAN stands next to him.

ANGLE ON

the MAN on the side of the road, and the woman. The man shovels dead rats out of a wheelbarrow and into a large pit. As John approaches he stops.

The WOMAN looks up and moves her parasol back slightly to view John.

                    WOMAN
          You are the new doctor.

A waft of burning smoke rises up from the rat pit.

                    JOHN
          Yes. Weiland, John Weiland.

                    WOMAN
          Living at the Wakefield house?

John nods.

                    WOMAN (CONT'D)
          We have always had a problem with
          rats in this town. How do you find
          the house?

                    JOHN
          It's well. Fine.

John smiles at her.

                    WOMAN
          And your wife?

                    JOHN
          My wife?

                    WOMAN
          Yes, your wife. And her sister too.
          Are they getting along fine?

                    JOHN
          Yes, they are. We are all getting
          along just fine, thank you.

The man pitches a shovel full of rats into
the pit.

                    WOMAN
          Perhaps they could come into town.
          We have a women's club there.

                    JOHN
          I'll mention it to them.

           WOMAN
Please.

            JOHN
Forgive me, but I have to be getting
on now. Good day to you.

           WOMAN
Good day.

John gets on his bicycle and continues on.

                        CUT TO:

CLOSE UP

of John, bicycling. He looks over his
shoulder to glance once more at the
strange picture: old herald and man with
vermin.

John looks back to the road, and continues
on.

                        CUT TO:

EXT. TREACHEROUS MOUNTAINS. DAY.

Jennie and Charlotte walk together along a
rocky path.

           CHARLOTTE
How long do you think you'll stay
now?

           JENNIE
However long you--

                    CHARLOTTE
          You do not need to stay because of
          me.

                    JENNIE
                    (firm)
          Charlotte.

                    CHARLOTTE
          And you do not need to stay here for
          John, either.

Jennie stops and reaches into her pocket.

                    JENNIE
          Listen. I've been waiting to give
          you this. I found it in my pocket
          the day after.

She hands Charlotte a tiny child's toy.
Jennie puts her hand up to her mouth.

Charlotte takes it in her hand. It is a
small thing against the barren desert
around them.

                    CHARLOTTE
          It's so strange that it can be so
          close to me, and I can suddenly feel
          nothing.

Jennie begins to cry.

                                        CUT TO:

INT. WAKEFIELD HOUSE. DAY.

The front door opens. John enters with a
plain brown bag of food.

Silence.

John closes the door behind him.

Suddenly there is the sound of tiny feet.

A child's feet. In the sitting room.

John immediately turns and steps into the sitting room.

                              CUT TO:

INT. SITTING ROOM. DAY.

The sofa is in the center of the room surrounded by palms and various chairs. Much like the library, it is a strange museum. Deep long shadows fall from the tall windows.

                    JOHN
          Charlotte?

The sitting room is silent.

John moves into the hallway.

Empty.

At the end of the hall, John notices the door to the side porch is open.

John moves down the hall to the door. He moves through it to the small porch.

The storage room door is cracked open.

                              CUT TO:

INT. STORAGE ROOM. DAY.

John opens the door.

Charlotte is inside going through large boxes of clothes. She glances to him, but says nothing. She continues to hold up the items and examine them.

> JOHN
> Did Jennie just come back through this hall?

> CHARLOTTE
> No. She's out back starting her garden.

> JOHN
> She's wasting her time. Hendricks said the land is useless. Nothing will grow.

> CHARLOTTE
> There are trunks full of old clothing in here. Maybe some things we can use. . . so much of it is rotted to dust. (beat) What a shame.

John stands in the doorway. He says nothing for a time.

> JOHN
> You should not be exerting yourself.

Charlotte ignores him and continues looking at the clothes.

John watches her sadly--and slightly angry--then turns. . . and exits the doorway.

> CUT TO:

EXT. FRONT PORCH. NIGHT.

WE PAN ACROSS THE DECK
Jennie wrestles with a large black hoop
dress on her lap. She attempts to pull out
the wires from the dress. Charlotte sits
next to her.

                    CHARLOTTE
          It's so quiet.

                    JENNIE
          Yes, strange for this time of year.
          Usually this kind of heat attracts
          so many bugs.

                    JOHN
          Oh.

John gets up and exits into the house.

                    JENNIE
          I don't think I can pull these out.
          They are sewn in too tightly.

Charlotte takes the dress from Jennie and
starts to look at it herself.

John comes back onto the porch.

                    JOHN
          Look at this.

John hands Jennie a parchment. Jennie
takes it and examines the writing.

                    JENNIE
          Me?

                    JOHN
          Yes.

Jennie looks down at the parchment.

                    JOHN (CONT'D)
          You studied French.

                    JENNIE
          Ages ago.

                    JOHN
          I found it tucked away in the
          library. I thought you might know
          what it is says.

                    JENNIE
          It's a lease. From. . .   1785.

                    JENNIE (cont.)
          I think.

                    JOHN
          The date I can make out myself.

                    CHARLOTTE
          John.

                    JENNIE
          A small furnished house...in
          Toulouse. The rest is...just legal.
          To tell you the truth, it's rather
          hard to read.

Jennie hands the paper back to John. John
takes it and begins to examine it himself.
He moves to the edge of the porch.

                    CHARLOTTE
          Well, I suppose we'll just have to
          make do with these, wear them as is.

                    JENNIE
          I wish that we could forage enough
          material in that house to make
          something... (to John) more modern.

                    CHARLOTTE
          Oh, but John. We did find a coat for
          you, but it's a bit worn.
          Jennie holds the dress at arm's
          length.

                    JENNIE
          This is the kind of dress Mother
          would have worn...every day of her
          life... What would she have done
          with it?

                    CHARLOTTE
          Turned it inside out and used it as
          two dresses.

They laugh.

                    JENNIE
          I think so.

                    CHARLOTTE
          (automatic-forgetting)
          Sarah?

John freezes.

Jennie stops what she is doing and reaches
her hands out to her sister.

Charlotte is instantly broken - stunned.

Their silence is interrupted by a piercing

HOWL.

Everyone freezes.

Then another wild dog howls.

And another.

And another.

John stares into the vast darkness. The sounds are coming from all around them.

Jennie and Charlotte stand up, alarmed.

John steps back from the top step of the porch.

> JOHN
> (to himself)
> I think we should go inside now.

                              CUT TO:

INT. JOHN AND CHARLOTTE'S ROOM. NIGHT. LATER.

Charlotte sits up in bed. Awake.

John sleeps beside her.

Charlotte pulls the covers away from her and quietly gets out of bed.

                              CUT TO:

INT. SEWING ROOM. NIGHT.

Charlotte closes the bedroom door and turns to the small door which leads up to the yellow wallpaper room.

She turns the key, opens it.

Charlotte lifts the lantern.

The stairs are illuminated.

Charlotte disappears through the door, and up the steps.

                                    CUT TO:

INT. JOHN AND CHARLOTTE'S ROOM. NIGHT.

John struggles with the blanket. He pulls it slightly towards him.

The blanket pulls in the opposite direction. Half asleep, he pulls again.

The covers slide quickly.

John turns over.

The bed is empty.

Groggy, he falls back asleep.

                                    CUT TO:

INT. THE YELLOW WALLPAPER ROOM. NIGHT.

Charlotte's lantern illuminates the room as she moves up the staircase. It is a strange and empty space. A rusted, metal bed. A single ornate desk.

The patterns of the wallpaper stretch in the flickering light of the flame.

Charlotte moves to the small desk and looks down to the scattered papers and an old ink well.

She backs up to the wall and leans against it, a curious expression covering her face.

> JENNIE O.C.
> There is something there. Behind.

CUT TO:

EXT. UNDER THE HOUSE. DAY.

John is underneath the porch, searching. He crawls around the brick piling that holds up the old structure. John struggles through a plot of bramble.

> JENNIE
> Do you see anything?

> JOHN
> No.

He crawls into the darkest corner beneath the house.

He falters--

> JOHN (CONT'D)
> Agh!

Steading himself, he squints to see a deep, wide gap in the earth.

Vines and tendrils wrap around the mouth and disappear into the pit.

> JENNIE
> What is it?

                         JOHN
          A well.

                         JENNIE
          What?

John leans in to hear a singing sound
ringing from deep inside the raw hole.

                         JENNIE
          John...what? What did you say?

John leans over and puts his hand down on
a SLIPPERY dead rat. He jerks back and up!
BANG.

John whacks his head on the rafters.

John scurries out of the crawl space. He
immediately goes to the grass and begins
to wipe off his hand. He turns and sees a
pail of water Jennie was washing the
windows with. He walks to it and sinks his
hands inside.

                         JENNIE (CONT'D)
          Are you okay? What happened?

                         JOHN
          Yes, there are rats alright.

                         JENNIE
          I knew I had heard something last
          night. I'll set out the traps then.
          They carry disease. We do not want
          them getting into the house.

                         JOHN
          All right.

John glances up to the window of the
yellow wallpaper room.

Charlotte moves past the window and vanishes into the recesses of the room.

CUT TO:

EXT. FRONT OF WAKEFIELD HOUSE. DAY.

A YOUNG MAN, a messenger, runs towards the house. He reaches the front door and knocks.

Charlotte opens the door.

The young man stands before her, flushed, excited.

> CHARLOTTE
> Yes?

> YOUNG MESSENGER
> Is the doctor here?

CUT TO:

EXT. STRETCH OF LAND. DAY.

John stands and watches the men. Everything is silent. If John's expression were a voice, it would say, 'I can't believe it's come down to this'.

The two men stand across from each other, guns held up beside their faces. The DUEL is about to begin.

The younger of the two duellists is PETER WARE. His expression is betrayed by his uncontrollable shaking. DAVID KILBOURNE, the older of the two, is serene, steady, even cocky.

An OLD MAN stands close to John.

> OLD MAN
> One, two, three, four, five.

A gunshot.

                                        CUT TO:

John sews up DAVID KILBOURNE. Young Peter is gushing with pride and relief.

> JOHN
> You know this is illegal. Not to mention stupid.

> OLD MAN
> Not out here, son.

The needle goes in to David's arm, up and down.

                                        CUT TO:

INT. SITTING ROOM. DAY.

ANGLE ON

a needle going up and down. Jennie sits at the sewing machine, altering an old shirt.

                                        CUT TO:

EXT. STRETCH OF LAND. DAY.

> DAVID
> Stupid. This, coming from the man who just moved into the Wakefields'.
> . . I would look hard first before casting stones, Doctor. . .

                    JOHN
          I'd look hard first before taunting
          a man who is pushing a needle into
          your arm.

                    PETER
          Then you like the house, Dr. Weiland?

The men laugh at their inside joke.

                    DAVID
          Find it cozy, do you?

John, more unsettled than before, looks to
them, confused.

He stops mending the arm.

                    OLD MAN
          Quiet yourselves, you stupid fools.

                    JOHN
               (to Peter)
          What do you mean by that sir?

                    OLD MAN
          Nothing. They mean nothing.

                    DAVID
          Pardon me, but I'm still bleeding.

John goes back to sewing the man.

                                        CUT TO:

INT. SEWING ROOM. DAY.

ANGLE ON

Jennie's back. We pull in to her as she
continues to sew. She swats something at
the back of her neck. After a minute, she

does it again.

Jennie stops.

She turns around.

Jennie CLOSE UP

as she stares forward, trying to see if something is there.

                                    CUT TO:

INT. THE YELLOW WALLPAPER ROOM. DAY.

Charlotte writes at a small writing desk. We can hear the scrawl of her fountain pen.

Sweat beads on her forehead. Slowly she wipes it away.

After a moment, Charlotte undoes the top of her dress. And pulls it away from her. It is an erotic movement.

She drops the upper portion of her dress to the floor. The white undergarment is drenched in sweat.

                                    CUT TO:

INT. LIBRARY. DAY.

John is showing Dr. Jack Everland a book.

DR. EVERLAND leans on John's desk. John stands beside him. The doctor is about fifty to sixty years old. He has long sideburns, a nicely trimmed mustache, and wears an impeccably tailored brown flannel suit. He is a symbol of the old world:

rich, and over-adorned.

                    DR. EVERLAND
          Yes, I think you have discovered a
          king's ransom here with these books.

Dr. Everland closes the book that John was
showing him.

                    JOHN
          Well, they're not mine.

                    DR. EVERLAND
          Nevertheless, I think they are
          splendid.

                    JOHN
          I wish you could stay longer Jack;
          we have plenty of room.

                    DR. EVERLAND
          Thank you, but I have to be off
          again this evening. I was simply
          passing near enough to make a stop,
          see how you were doing.

                    JOHN
          I'm glad you did.

                    DR. EVERLAND
          So am I.

He sets the book down.

                    DR. EVERLAND (CONT'D)
          You know John, you do not look well.
          I was wondering if you knew that.

                    JOHN
          How do you mean?

                    DR. EVERLAND
          You look tired, and so do the women.

                    JOHN
          As you can imagine, we have not
          exactly been eating or sleeping
          well.

                    DR. EVERLAND
          You've all had a great deal of
          misfortune.

John moves to the other side of the room.

                    DR. EVERLAND
          Is there anything that I can do?

                    JOHN
          No, no Jack, you've done enough.

John walks around the desk, crosses his
arms, and looks out the window.

Dr. Everland says nothing. He watches
John.

                    DR. EVERLAND
          John? . . .

John turns to him.

                    DR. EVERLAND (CONT'D)
          I may have been your professor ten
          years ago, but I've been your friend
          for   almost as long. Tell me what
          is on your mind?

There is a long silence.

                    JOHN
          We were together... behind the house
          when the fire broke out.

The doctor waits.

> JOHN (CONT'D)
> Jennie was gone. It was early
> evening. When we got back, I ran
> through the front door. Everything
> was in flames, but. . . I ran
> upstairs. I couldn't help her; my
> baby was on fire... I couldn't reach
> her, Jack. I swear to God, I couldn't
> reach her.

John turns and looks at Dr. Everland.

> DR. EVERLAND
> I am sorry son.

> JOHN
> I do not even know how it began. I
> didn't know--

> DR. EVERLAND
> And how is Charlotte coping with
> this?

> CUT TO:

INT. JOHN AND CHARLOTTE'S ROOM. DAY.

CLOSE UP

of Charlotte. She sits and stares out the
window.

> JOHN O.C.
> I have known Charlotte since we were
> children, and there wasn't a moment
> of my life that I did not know I
> would spend the rest of my life with
> her, because she was so filled with

life. Now everything I thought I
knew I do not understand. (beat) And
I do not understand her.

                              CUT TO:

INT. LIBRARY. DAY.

EXTREME CLOSE UP

of Dr. Everland. His face is shrouded in
shadow, only his profile is illuminated.
He is the sage of a dream.   .   .
whispering.

                    DR. EVERLAND
          Yes you do.

                              CUT TO:

END OF EXCERPT.

Director Logan Thomas on the set of
The Yellow Wallpaper.

REFERENCES

Beauvoir, Simone De. 1952. *The Second Sex: The classic manifesto of the liberated woman*. New York: Alfred A . Knopf.

Chopin, Kate. *The Awakening*. 1976. New York: W.W. Norton & Company, Inc. Cully, Margaret (ed.).

Gilman, Charlotte Perkins. 1990. *The Living of Charlotte Perkins Gilman*. Madison, Wisconsin: The University of Wisconsin Press. Williams, Andrew L. (gen. ed.). Introduction by Lane, Ann J.

Melendy, Mary R., M.D., Ph.D. 1901. *Perfect Womanhood for Maidens – Wives – Mothers*. Copyright by Boland, K.T.

Shelley, Mary Wollstonecraft. 1988. *Frankenstein or The Modern Prometheus*. NY, NY: Portland House Illustrated Classics Division. Booss, Claire (series ed.). Foreward by Shapiro, Ellen S.

Stoker, Bram. 1975. *Dracula. The Annotated Dracula*. New York: Clarkson N. Potter, Inc. Wolf, Leonard (ed.).

Stetson, Charles Walter. 1985. Endure: The Diaries of Charles Walter Stetson. Philadelphia: Temple University Press. Hill, Mary Armfield (ed.).

Poe, Edgar Allan.1983. *Edgar Allan Poe: Greenwich Unabridged Library Classics*. New York: Chatham River Press. Foreward by Perry, Alix.

Vertinsky, Patricia A. 1994. *The Eternally Wounded Woman: Women, Doctors, and Exercise in the Late Nineteenth Century*. Manchester, USA. Manchester University Press.